Tales of the Were ~ Redstone Clan

Magnus

BIANCA D'ARC

DEDICATION

First of all, special thanks to my friend, Peggy McChesney for the moral support and helpful commentary. You are one in a million!

This book is dedicated to my family, and especially my paternal grandmother – a woman I never met because a bad gall bladder ended her life prematurely. I now have a new appreciation for what she went through all those years ago, way before I was born, and a new respect for modern medicine. Why? Because in the middle of finishing this book, my gall bladder finally made itself known in a very difficult way.

It had to come out and now I'm on the mend. Something my grandmother never got a chance to do. Instead, she lived with the pain and discomfort I now realize was caused by my bum gall bladder for years. From all accounts, I would have loved this grandmother I never knew. I wish I'd had a chance to get to know her, and I thank the surgeon and doctors who made sure I'm here now to finish this book and hopefully write many more.

I feel as if I've gotten a second chance and a bit of a restart. With any luck, things will only get better from this day forward for me, and I wish that for all of you as well.

CHAPTER ONE

Hunger.

Endless hunger. And pain.

The sadistic bastard that held her captive and forced Miranda to bleed for him was keeping her on a knife's edge of existence. She'd lost track of how long she'd been locked in the cage with silver bars. Bars that burned her if she dared touch them.

And she had dared. Many times. She'd tried her hardest to get out of the cage time and time again, to no avail. She had burns all over her hands from the times she'd tried to break the bonds meant solely to hold immortals. And burns all over her body from the times she'd been too weak to move away after he'd made her bleed for his disgusting evil magic.

Miranda had never succumbed to evil. She wasn't about to start now. It stole a part of her soul that a human mage had captured her and was taking her blood to fuel his dark magic. She had decided early on in her immortal existence that she would not fall to evil, no matter what had been done to her. No matter that she now could walk only at night and had to live off the blood of other beings. No matter what. She would serve the Light. She would not turn to the dark side. Even if that's what most people thought of her and her kind. Even if that's what her maker had intended.

The bastard. He'd been almost as bad as the bastard that now held her captive. To them, she was just a plaything. A toy for their amusement. A tool to be used as they saw fit. That kind of man didn't stop to consider what she wanted. What she thought. What she believed in. And that had been her maker's downfall. Perhaps somehow, she'd still find a way to prevail over the sick bastard who held her in a cage.

A *cage* for Goddess' sake. As if she was some kind of animal. She'd show him an animal if he ever came close enough for her to strike. A damn dangerous animal with sharp teeth and claws.

But every time he got near, his magic held her at bay. Someday though… She lived for the day he made a mistake.

Meanwhile, she'd watch and learn. She'd keep her eyes open during her moments of lucidity. She'd already heard things. Things that made her worry about the future—if she had a future, that is.

She had to stay positive. Even when the madman who held her captive raved. She had to believe that someday, somehow, he'd make a mistake that she could exploit. Even if he did claim to have powerful friends.

Venificus. The stuff of legend. Bad legends of dark days when the fate of all beings in this realm had been at a very dangerous tipping point. The forces of Light had won that battle, according to the ancient histories, but it seemed that time of danger was coming again. At least to hear this stinking human mage tell it. He raved about how they were actively working to bring back a creature of evil reputation— Elspeth, Destroyer of Worlds.

She'd almost achieved the chaos she wanted the last time she'd walked in this realm hundreds of years ago. Her evil had been stopped at great cost and she'd been banished to the forgotten realms where, it was hoped, she would learn the error of her ways over millennia.

But nobody had told Miranda that there were nutjobs like this guy trying to bring her back. According to her captor, agents of the *Venificus* were trying to breach the barriers between realms to pull that ancient fey bitch back through to this world from her place of exile.

Never mind that the *Venifucus*—the group formed from the loyal followers of Elspeth so long ago—had been thought to be gone for centuries. Apparently they were back in a big way and they were trying to bring their leader back. Crazy SOB's that they were.

Miranda would have been freaking out even more if she'd had the energy. As it was, when she surfaced for rare moments of lucidity—moments that were becoming rarer all the time as her starvation and blood loss worsened—she felt something like panic set in as she thought about what kind of effect bringing the Destroyer of Worlds back to the mortal realm would have. It would be the next best thing to Armageddon. Maybe the end of the world as they knew it.

If she had just a little more energy, and an opportunity, she'd break out of her cage and warn people. Tony, the Master of this area, needed to know about this dark mage. If anyone could stop him, Tony could. She knew the Master to be a man of honor. Unlike her maker. And very unlike the bastard who had put her in a cage of silver.

She feared that one day, he would drain her dry. If he did that, she wouldn't be able to come back. Not even her so-called immortal powers could save her from the final death then. She'd learned over the years that even vampires could be killed in a couple of ways. The old stake through the heart worked. Silver and severe blood loss could do it too.

He'd already exposed her to the poisonous metal, though it would have to actually be in her blood stream in order to kill her outright. Just touching the surface of her skin, all it did was burn her. Over and over. Causing severe pain. Not pleasant—and possibly disfiguring—but not quite lethal.

The blood loss though… That could be a problem. He kept bleeding her and not feeding her, not allowing her to recover between bleeds. Eventually, he'd take her last drop and with it, her life.

She sensed he was building up to something. Each time he

got a little bolder, a little more demanding, a little greedier. Each time, she slipped closer to oblivion. And sometimes—just sometimes—she almost hoped he'd go too far and end her pain for good.

She tried different things to conserve herself as much as possible. She'd learned how to shapeshift earlier than most of her kind. It was a talent she prided herself on. She could take the form of many different animals, but she hadn't yet mastered the ability to shift into mist. That would have been really helpful in her current situation, but that particular skill took centuries to perfect and she hadn't been shapeshifting long enough to turn herself into floating molecules. If she ever got out of here though, she'd work on it until she had it down pat. She wasn't going to be put in this kind of situation ever again.

Each time he came to her now, she shapeshifted into something else. Something with claws that could hurt him. She dreamed of making him bleed. Except for the first time, he never got close enough, and after she'd slashed him that once, he was always careful to shield himself with sinister magic she could not pierce.

A new strategy came to her almost by accident. She shapeshifted into something smaller than her real size and the sorcerer was very angry. In the smaller body, she had less blood for him to drain. She kept trying to go smaller and smaller each time he came to her after that, and his anger knew no bounds.

Good. She loved the tiny bit of rebellion, and kept trying to go smaller until she'd finally hit upon the form of a baby bear. It was as small as she could go in her present state, and the claws gave her some advantage, even if she was kind of puny.

Then one night, he came for her again and she knew this would be the last time. He had that evil chalice with him. He'd been working on the thing for a long time. She had a feeling that when he finished torturing cats and other animals, he would come for her and put the last of her blood into his despicable vessel. What he planned to do with that kind of power she had no idea, but she knew it couldn't be anything good. Not this man. Not with blood magic.

When he came to her cage, she steeled herself, shifting shape into the baby bear form he hated so much. At least in this form, he wouldn't be getting that much blood, even if he killed her this time. And her death would be faster. A mercy, she thought, after so long in captivity at this lunatic's hands.

He forced her into the energy circle he'd laid out on the floor of his workroom. Once inside, she was unable to move, to hear or smell anything outside the evil circle. She was trapped within. Unable to reach forward and claw his eyes out or sink her teeth into her carotid artery and end his evil while feeding her blazing hunger. He'd starved her for so long to keep her as docile as possible. She was about to lose her mind with the hunger that rode her.

And then the pain began. With magical strokes of his evil blade, he cut her from a few feet away. He never got close enough for her to strike, and he kept her within a tight circle of his power, controlling her. She bled while he directed the chalice under her, catching her life's essence into the tainted vessel.

She felt herself fading and almost welcomed oblivion. She'd suffered for a long time at this bastard's hands. She craved vengeance, but she didn't think she was going to get it in this lifetime.

And then there was a strange man looking at her from outside the circle. A man, and a woman too. He had the looks of a shifter, but his eyes glowed with magic. A mage then. Or something she had never met before. The woman with him was different too. She looked human, but carried herself like a magic user. She pulled the tools of the sorcerer from her bag and began placing ritual objects around the perimeter of the circle that trapped Miranda.

More magic? Miranda felt rage pulse through her. They were talking, but she couldn't hear them. Her senses couldn't penetrate the evil power of the circle in which she was trapped. And the mage who had held her captive for so very long was not in the room. When had that happened? Where had he gone? And who were these new people?

The couple looked at her and seemed to be debating something. Her captor was still nowhere to be seen. Had these two broken in to steal from him? Were they after her? Did they want to use her blood for their own purposes?

Miranda was fuzzy at best after being held captive so long, but she vowed she would not go quietly. She would fight them in whatever way she could. She would do her utmost to get free and take down as many of the bad guys as she could on her way out. This might be her only chance.

Hope bubbled within her tired heart. Hope and lust for vengeance…and blood. She needed blood. Needed it so bad. Like a junkie needing a fix. *Worse* than a junkie. She needed it to live. To be strong enough to get away and hide before the sun rose.

She would take any blood she could get at this point. Animal, human, whatever. She was so depleted, she was almost insane with the pounding thirst that drove her. She knew she was not rational, but she didn't care. If the opportunity arose, she would feed, and if she killed, so be it. She owed the bastard who'd captured her as much mayhem as she could deliver. And if he wasn't available, she'd have to exact her vengeance on his friends.

Surely, these were some of his people, whom he'd let in. *Venificus* agents. Friends of her captor. Enemies. How else could they have penetrated to the heart of his lair?

She crouched in her baby bear form. They seemed cautious of her. Well, they should be. The moment they made a mistake, she'd make her move.

Miranda watched as the female finished placing her crystals at the four cardinal points around the circle. They conferred over something in the woman's hand and then the man came closer, right up to the edge of the circle that held her. He dropped some kind of pinkish crystal grains straight across the circle's barrier. She felt it fall, and then she made her move.

Using the last of her energy, fueled by hunger and rage, she shifted shape as she launched herself at the man with the glowing blue eyes. She took her human form, but left her hands tipped with claws, scratching deep gouges in the man's hide as she took him by surprise.

He was fast though, and had good reflexes. And she was weak with hunger and on the verge of losing her mind. She felt fury rise along with the thirst. She needed his blood and that gave her strength. She positioned her fangs over his pulse and was about to strike.

"Miranda, no!"

The voice made her pause. Something in her recognized that voice, even through her blood haze and fury. The voice made her heart weep. A voice from her past she never thought to hear again.

She looked up and met the golden gaze of the man her heart had never forgotten. The man her soul cried out for. The man she could never have for her own.

"Miranda!" he called her name once more.

Mag. Oh, dear Goddess. Mag was here.

Either that, or she was hallucinating. She tilted her head, wondering if she had finally snapped over the line of insanity or if this was some kind of cruel hoax being perpetrated by her captor. Or worse…if it was real.

Sweet Mother of All.

She let go of the blue eyed man as Mag approached her cautiously. She didn't even notice as the man slumped and moved away, helped by the woman he'd been with. She only had eyes for Magnus Redstone. She tried to move toward him, but she was so weak. She couldn't walk much.

"Careful, Mag!" Another male voice called from the doorway. She heard it, but she couldn't look away from Magnus. Her One. The lover from her past she could never reclaim. He'd broken her heart though he'd never meant to do so.

"It's okay. This is Miranda. She's a friend of mine." He

spoke to the others in the room with them, though his gaze never left hers. "Sweetheart, what have they done to you?" His voice dropped low and she could hear his dismay in the way his voice broke.

Then he held out his arms and she couldn't deny the impulse. She wanted to feel his touch, his arms around her...one last time before she left this realm.

"Magnus?" He felt so good. So solid. If this was a dream, she never wanted to wake up.

She was so weak, she couldn't really regulate what was left of her power. She knew her voice held the vampire magic that had come to her after her turning. Usually, she could control it. She wouldn't use that power over Mag. But she had no strength. And very little blood left. She was as close to leaving this realm as she'd ever been.

"I'm here, sweetheart. I've got you." His arms tightened around her and she trembled as he held her tight against his hard body. She rested her head in the crook of his shoulder. So close to temptation...but she'd never hurt Mag. She'd die before she hurt him.

"She needs to feed," the woman's whisper came from behind her. She sounded so afraid. Didn't she realize Miranda would never harm her One?

"I know." Mag's deep voice rumbled against her and Miranda loved the sensation. His broad hand cupped the back of her head and she felt so safe. Safer than she had in so long. She'd been held in a cage for so very long...

He guided her head, pushing her lips toward his throat, her fangs toward the source of his pounding pulse. Oh, no.

She couldn't help herself. She was *so* hungry. And she'd missed Mag so much. She nuzzled her lips against his skin, letting her tongue out to taste the unforgettable salt of his skin.

Her fangs needed to sink into him. She needed to taste his essence. She knew she was starved, but she didn't just want to drink to slake her thirst. She wanted that forbidden taste of Mag. *Her* Mag. The One who'd got away. The One she had pushed away for his own good.

They could never be together. She would have to console herself with the few short memories she had of him for the rest of her days.

But Miranda knew she was still bleeding out. These moments might very well be her last. If that was the way it was going to be, she wanted one last taste of Mag's essence—his amazingly wild shifter blood. She'd only tasted it once and it had ruined her for all others. But that was okay. Fate hadn't ever been kind to Miranda. Not since the day she'd been turned and had to leave all she knew behind. All because of one man's greed.

Not this man. Not the man who held her with all the gentleness in him. Never Mag. No, Mag was the one bright spot in her immortal existence. And the cruelest temptation that could ever be devised by man or nature.

She bit into his flesh, taking the most delicate care not to hurt him. She would never hurt him. Not on purpose.

The flavor of his blood filled her with longing she knew could never be fulfilled. He tasted like her mate. Her One and only. But he also tasted of shifter—the wild flavor of the woodlands and desert. And the incredible magic that filled his being. It brought on a sense of euphoria as his power filled the empty places in her. Not to overflowing. She was too blood-starved. It would take a lot more than the gentle sips of his essence that she allowed herself.

But she wouldn't—couldn't—do that to him. She would never take so much as to hurt him. All she wanted was one last drink of him to take with her into the next realm. One last happy thought. One last magical moment with the only man she would ever love.

She lifted her fangs out of his neck and sealed the little punctures as best she could in her weakened condition. She heard the people in the room around them moving and talking, though she let their words flow around her without really listening. All that mattered to her was the man who held her with such gentleness. Who gave her his blood so freely and with such selflessness when she was so starved for it—and for him—though he'd never know how much it had hurt her to leave him.

"I've missed you, Miranda," he whispered so that only she could hear him. The emotion in his eyes when he moved back far enough to look down at her mirrored her own feelings.

She knew her vampiric magic was affecting him. His eyes held a bit of that glazed euphoria her bite usually brought to her human prey. She almost regretted that, but she was glad she'd left him with good feelings, not bad. That was important to her.

He didn't give her a chance to say anything before he scooped her weak body up into his arms and strode out of the room past everyone. He didn't stop to talk. He didn't even glance at the people they passed. He just walked, single-mindedly, out into the night with her in his arms.

"Where are you taking me?" Miranda's voice was weak, her grip on him loose as Mag carried her out into the night.

His heart had nearly stopped beating when he'd caught her distinct scent of cinnamon and roses inside that despicable house. He'd rushed inside and into the front room, which had been set up as some kind of magic-working chamber of horrors, just in time to see Miranda transform from a small bear cub into her true form—a vampiress.

He'd known her for just over two years. They'd had a fling, if that's what you call a passionate night of once-in-a-lifetime sex followed by the woman fleeing before dawn, never to be seen again.

He'd never forgotten her. In fact, he hadn't been with another woman since Miranda. She had ruined him for anyone else, and he didn't know what to do about it.

Mag had been dismayed to realize that she was his mate. A vampiress. It couldn't be, but these past two years of celibacy had proven otherwise. No other woman would do for him. His heart, the cougar that shared his soul, and his body only wanted Miranda.

But it *really* couldn't be. There were taboos about shifters and vamps getting together. Mag hadn't spoken of his dilemma with anyone. Not even his big brother Grif, Alpha of the Redstone Clan. Mag knew without asking that his attachment to a vamp would go down like a lead balloon. It just wasn't done.

"Mag?" Miranda whispered as he headed straight for his car.

He thanked the Goddess he'd taken the convertible tonight. It would be easy to lift his precious burden into the passenger seat without jarring her any more than necessary.

"I'm taking you home, Miranda. To my home. You'll be safe there for the day. I have a light-proofed room."

"You do?" Her tone was both weary and suspicious. He was sure if she had been more alert she would have been asking him all sorts of questions about why a cougar shapeshifter would just happen to have a light-proofed room in his home. It wasn't for him. He certainly didn't need it.

But how could he explain that he'd gotten to work on light-proofing his house the day after Miranda had left him. He'd known it was impossible for them to be mates, but his heart and the big cat that shared his soul had refused to listen. Some part of him still held out the forlorn hope that somehow he would see her again—and have her in his home.

He lifted her over the side of the car and placed her gently into the bucket seat. He didn't care about the grime or blood on her clothes, though it pained him to see his beloved in such a state. She'd been held captive for who knew how long—and she'd nearly died tonight.

Mag had to believe that the Lady was watching over them. Of all the places for him to be on this particular night... It was kismet that he was here, now, in time to save her.

The way she'd attacked that guy Slade... That had been bad. Mag shuddered to think about what would have happened if he hadn't been there and she hadn't responded to his voice. His brothers—or maybe even Slade or the priestess he was so cozy with—would have had to hurt Miranda. They might've even finished what the evil mage had started, and killed her.

She would have died. The mere thought of it nearly broke Mag's battered heart.

"Most of my house is light-proofed, sweetheart," he admitted as he placed the seatbelt around her. He wasn't taking any chances with her safety...from now on.

Her dazed eyes met his. It was clear she was in a lot of pain and still seemed very out of it, but she focused on him, her lovely blue eyes meeting his.

"Why would you do that? You are all that's most perfect about the sun. Why would you need to hide from it?"

"I don't," he admitted, pausing at the side of the car, bent over her. "But I always hoped I'd see you again."

There it was. Mag had put himself out there as much as he dared for the moment. She wasn't pulling away. In fact, judging by the way her expression softened, she liked what he'd said.

A frail hand rose to cup his cheek and he turned his head, placing a soft kiss in her palm. His heart was almost whole for the first time in over two years.

"I always hoped I'd see you again too, even though I know this can never be."

"I think I'm through playing by the rules, Miranda." He had to state his intentions. He wanted her to know that he was drawing a line in the sand. "I won't leave you like this. You need time and space to heal. I have both—a place for you to recover and blood that will speed your healing. Whatever comes after...we'll deal with as it comes. Right now, I think the Lady put me here on this night to help you. Who are we to argue with fate?"

She looked skeptical as she lowered her trembling hand. "I don't know what to think right now. All I know is that I need to get away from here." She looked back over her shoulder toward the house of terror where she had been imprisoned. "Take me somewhere else, Mag."

Her plea nearly broke his heart. Mag leaned down to place a kiss on her forehead.

"You're free now, sweetheart. And you're not alone. Anybody wants to mess with you right now, they'll have to go through me. And that just ain't gonna happen. Trust me on that."

"I do trust you, Mag. With my life," she whispered. But he knew she hadn't trusted him with the most important thing of all—her heart.

CHAPTER TWO

Magnus Redstone pushed the sports car to its limits getting Miranda home. She was fading in and out of consciousness and he worried for her. He needed to get her to his house and check her injuries. He wouldn't stop worrying until he got a much better look at how badly she was hurt.

He had a place on the outskirts of the housing development they'd build just for shifters on Clan lands, but he didn't spend a lot of time there lately. No, most of his time was spent at a little hideaway he'd bought in the desert, on a wide stretch of open land populated only by cactus and the occasional snake or scorpion. He headed there now, glad that it was actually closer than the shifter neighborhood from this particular angle.

He hadn't told his brothers the details about his place in the desert. Not that it was any big secret or anything. He had just wanted a project of his own to help him decompress, and the isolation had helped him cope after meeting and then losing Miranda that first time. This was the home he'd light-proofed and made ready in the almost impossible expectation that somehow, someday, she'd return to him.

Mag would give anything for her to have come to him on her own. He'd tried to find her that morning after she left, but she had made a clean getaway. There was no scent trail for him to follow. He'd also looked for her using modern tools—the internet and public records—but she remained hidden and eventually he'd had to concede defeat. It ate him up inside to have given up.

The fact that she was here now sent a thrill of victory through the primitive part of his brain, but he would have rather had her return healthy. He hated the fact that she was too weak to remain conscious. He hated the fact that she was injured and had suffered untold horrors at the hands of a *Venifucus* mage. He would give anything to take all that pain away from her—for it to have never happened in the first place.

But he couldn't change the past. No more than he could change the fact that she was a vampire and he was a shifter. Or the fact that she was, without doubt, his mate.

It was impossible. Forbidden. Frowned upon by both races. Just not done.

Mag had researched it. He hadn't been able to find a vamp-shifter mating since the days of Elspeth. Only during the threat of those dark times had the taboo been lifted and a few shifters had been allowed to mate with a few very special vampires.

Shifter blood was like a drug to vamps. It gave them the strength and cunning of the shifter. It was a rare thing for any shifter to willingly allow a bloodletter to drink from them. In the modern era, vamps-shifter matings were intensely discouraged so the vampire of the pair wouldn't have unlimited access to that extra-magical blood.

For one thing, the vampire Masters and Mistresses of each region didn't want the competition. They held their positions of power over the rest of their kind by being the strongest— usually that also meant they were old and had lots of experience under their belts. For another, the shifter community didn't like to give any particular vampire that much power. The bloodsuckers were plenty strong enough on their own without the addition of potent shifter blood.

"Where are we?" Miranda's voice was weaker than before. She'd been fading in and out since he'd put her in the car and it worried him.

"Almost there, sweetheart. Hang on for me. I'll have you inside and under cover soon. I promise."

"Okay, Mag." Silence followed them through the night as the wind whipped through his hair. "I missed you."

Only his sharp shifter hearing picked up her quiet, slurred words over the wind as she fell back into unconsciousness. Damn. The woman knew how to get to him. Her unguarded admission touched him deep inside, drawing an answering ache to match that which he'd heard in her voice.

Every moment of every day, he'd missed her too. In his bed. In his house. The house he'd prepared for her presence though she'd never set foot in it before. Even though they'd only spent that one terrible, fantastic night together.

She had shredded his heart that night—or more accurately, that morning when he'd woken without her. She'd fled in the night while he slept and taken his heart with her.

The practical side of him knew she had left to save them both from the wrath of their respective peoples. But the emotional side of him knew only that he'd found his mate—at last—and she'd left him. His inner cougar had been inconsolable. His human heart had been broken beyond anyone's ability to repair it. Anyone but Miranda, that is.

And now, here she was. In his car. Soon to be, in his house. Their house. The house he had refitted especially for her.

He pulled into the drive a few minutes later and hit the button that would raise the garage door. He parked the convertible while the door slid down, encasing the garage in darkness, but it was okay. He had excellent night vision.

Mag did a quick scan of the security screen before disarming the alarm system. Everything was as it should be in the house and now it was even more so, with Miranda finally here. He lifted her out of the car as gently as possible and brought her inside through the entrance from the garage, securing it behind him. The house was filled with the latest gadgetry in every respect—including security.

He'd learned a thing or two from his older brother Steve, who handled security for the entire Clan as well as their family business, Redstone Construction. Steve had been a Green Beret, as had their eldest brother, Grif. Both of them knew more about personal security than most, and Mag had taken every lesson they'd been willing to share to heart. He'd outfitted his hideaway with the most state of the art stuff he could get and installed every bit of it himself.

This house had been the project that had kept him sane while missing his mate. It wasn't easy for shifters to be parted from their destined mate. In fact, it could drive most insane. Mag had turned to his work to give him something to focus on beside his pain at losing Miranda. He'd sunk himself into the projects the construction company had going during his working hours, then come here and spent the rest of his time building and improving this little nest out in the desert.

His brothers hadn't known what he did with his spare time. Grif had probably realized he was troubled, but he hadn't asked. Grif knew well enough that cougars needed to prowl alone from time to time. Bob, a few years younger than Mag, had learned the hard way not to ask what was wrong. They'd mixed it up a time or two—especially right after that night with Miranda. It was almost as if Bob had known Mag needed to blow off some steam and had sort of volunteered to be his sparring partner.

Bob was good like that, but it was Matt, their youngest brother, that Mag really needed to talk to now. Matt knew vampires. He was close with a few of the most powerful bloodletters in the Napa Valley. Mag had broached the subject delicately a few times over the past two years and he'd learned quite a bit. Including how to fix up the house so his mate would be comfortable.

But the part that eluded him was how they could *be* mates in the first place. Surely the Mother of All wouldn't have allowed it if it wasn't meant to be? Mag had always placed a great deal of his trust in the Lady he served. He had seen Her influence in the lives of his family for many years, and when tragedy struck, She was always there for them.

The latest horror of his mother's brutal murder had been an attack by the forces of darkness, but Kate, the Clan's priestess, was on the case with another of Her servants—a newcomer with so much magic, he glowed, according to his cousin Keith, who could actually *see* magic. So although bad things had happened—really bad things—Mag still had faith. After all, in tracking down the murderers, he'd discovered Miranda.

For it was the same evil mage who had somehow captured and then tortured Miranda for who knew how long, who had been part of the team that had killed Mag's mother. Grif was leading the search, with Slade's help. The family had been in disarray before Slade had shown up. He'd been sent by the Lords of all *were* to help, and so far, he'd produced amazing results.

They'd taken down the male mage tonight and with any luck, his female accomplice wouldn't be too hard to find. Mag would be there for his family when they needed him, but for right now, Miranda needed him more.

Poor Miranda. Held captive by an evil madman. Mag felt sick just thinking about it. The only things that helped were knowing they'd rescued her, and having her in his arms. He would take care of her from now on. He'd see that she recovered her full strength and that something like this could never happen again.

Mag carried Miranda directly into the master suite's attached bath. To say the room was a study in decadence was understating it. He'd installed marble everywhere, with a giant tub big enough for two. Wide sinks and vanity space. Sculpted marble everywhere in a sandy color with desert and cougar motifs. It was a wild place with discrete arrangements of tropical plants that gave it the feeling of a rainforest when the shower misted water into the air. A little piece of the rainforest in the middle of the desert. Mag liked the contrast.

But all he was interested in at the moment was the giant, walk-in shower he'd put at one end of the room. It had a sculpted bench along the back. The soft edges wouldn't hurt Miranda as he undressed her, cleaned her up and inspected her wounds.

She was still mostly out of it, so he leaned her against the wall and began by tugging off her pants. She wore no shoes. The bastard that had held her had kept her barefoot. Or maybe she'd lost her shoes at one point, and the bastard had never replaced them. After all, it was easy to keep something dangerous in a cage. It was another thing entirely to open the cage and hope the dangerous creature wouldn't bite your arm off.

The mage probably hadn't dared let her out of her cage unless his magical barriers were fully in place. Even the most powerful of magic users couldn't maintain those circles of power indefinitely. Or so Mag had heard. He'd tried to learn all he could about vamps after his one night stand with Miranda, but he'd also gained a few tidbits about magic users while he'd been asking subtle questions of all and sundry.

Her legs were as long and lean as Mag remembered from their one night together. He'd loved having her slim thighs wrapped around him, her pale skin a stark contrast against his tanned bronze. She was everything that was elegant and beautiful in his world. He almost wept at the pleasure of having her here, in the house he had so lovingly prepared for her.

Her legs were a little scratched up, but otherwise sound, so he moved upward and tried to tug the ragged shirt off her arms. She fought him a little until her eyes opened and she recognized him. Her fight ceased and she seemed dazzled by the sight of him.

"Mag?" She sounded confused and he grew more worried about her condition. Miranda was one of the strongest women he knew despite her fragile appearance.

"I'm here, sweetheart. Just let me get these ruined things off you so you can get clean. Does it hurt anywhere?" He kept his tone gentle, even as he pried her clenched hands away from the ragged edges of her top.

She had shifted back into her clothes as they had been when she'd assumed the form of the bear cub. Vampires who could shapeshift did it in a different way than most animal shapeshifters. *Weres* couldn't take their clothing into the shift with them. Mag had to either get naked before he shifted or keep replacing his torn clothing. But Miranda had all that vampire magic at her disposal. She could shift from fully clothed human to fur-covered bear and back again.

Whatever she'd been wearing when she went into the shift came back with her on the other side, as long as she willed it. Or so Matt had claimed when Mag had quizzed his younger brother on the topic. As it happened, Matt knew a young vampiress who was learning how to shapeshift from her mate, and Matt had a few funny stories to tell about her attempts to become a cat. According to Matt, her mate had suggested she try for a cat assuming she'd become a cougar like Matt. Instead, she'd opted for a tiny housecat, much to the amusement of all concerned. From then on, Matt said, her mate was careful to be a lot more specific when he made suggestions.

Miranda moaned when he tugged her arm free of the ripped up sweater she had worn. When he straightened her arm and saw the sheer number of cuts, both old and new, she whimpered.

"What did he do to you?" he whispered, unable to hide his dismay.

Her arm was a mass of scars, burns, and open slices that were bleeding sluggishly. The burns were a sickly black and green—caused by silver, Mag thought. He'd seen what looked like a dully gleaming silver cage in that room of horrors and he'd smelled the sickening tang of the poisonous metal in the air. The cuts, on the other hand, looked as if she'd been tortured—sliced over and over by a sharp blade.

The dark fabric of her sweater had hidden the dark flow of her blood. Normally, vampires could heal themselves with a thought, but it was clear now to Mag that Miranda had been systematically drained of her blood—and her magic—over what had to be months, or possibly years. His heart ached for her suffering. She didn't have enough strength left to even close the cuts, much less eliminate the scars as he knew she could have done. His concern over her state of health grew.

He tried not to move too fast for her abused limbs as he tugged her other arm free of the sweater and then lifted the ragged remnants of it over her head. He did his best not to let his shock show when he saw the gouges in her skin all over her breasts and neck. She still wore a lacy bra and panties, but it was clear the mage had hurt any inch of skin he could access with his evil magic.

"What made these marks, my love?" he asked gently, needing to know, but also dreading the answer.

"Magic. Blades." She sighed heavily as he hit the button that would start the computerized shower at a low level. He adjusted the temperature to something soothing and peaceful, regulating the flow of the jets to a steady, gentle spray. "Magic blades."

"Did he touch you?"

Miranda smiled, but it was a deadly, cold thing. Then her eyes sparked and he saw a glimmer of his former lover in her gaze. "He tried, but he learned quickly not to get too near my cage."

"How long were you there?" he asked, but she was losing strength again. Mag quickly lifted her into the soothing spray, washing away the blood and grime, not caring that he was getting soaked. He was fully clothed, but he didn't care. All that mattered was Miranda.

She didn't answer his question. She was so weak, but he knew what she needed. She needed blood and he was the closest donor. She'd already taken some from him earlier, but he knew it wasn't enough. He guided her head into the crook of his shoulder while the water sprayed gently around them. Running his hands over the undamaged places on her skin, he tried to wash away the evidence of what had been done to her.

"You need to drink, sweetheart," he said gently, placing her on her feet. She was the perfect height for him. Her chin rested in the crook of his neck, giving her easy access to the blood she so desperately needed.

"Don't want to hurt you," she murmured, arguing without much heat.

"You won't. I trust you."

She found the strength to pull back and look into his eyes. "You shouldn't," she said very seriously. "I'm not in control right now. I've been starved for too long. I don't trust my own mind. There were moments when…" she paused, swallowing hard, "…when I thought I was going mad. I still might be. I don't trust myself."

"Trust me then, Miranda," he whispered, needing to help her, to give her back some of the self-confidence that had been stolen from her. "I believe in you. You won't hurt me. You need strength, and my blood is the most potent around here at the moment. Take some. Lean on me. I'll take care of you. Always."

He cupped the back of her head, guiding her toward his neck and even though he sensed she still wanted to protest, she eventually gave in to the thirst he knew had to be riding her. She bit, taking care to be gentle, as he knew she would. She had always treated him gently, with what he hoped was caring, if not love.

He hated the thought that he might be the only one feeling the mating bond between them. He didn't know what vamps felt for their mates—or if she felt it for him. He hoped, but she'd never said anything. He'd taken her flight from his bed after that one night they'd spent together as a sort of mute confirmation that their connection had scared her as much as it had him. But over the two years since that incredible night, he'd learned to respect the bond—to thirst for the closeness it promised. It had been a hard lesson. One full of frustration and anger at himself for being such a coward on that first and only night. He should've said something right then and there, but he hadn't dared. He'd thought he would have time to process the incredible changes meeting his mate had begun in his life, but when he woke up, she was gone.

She bit into his neck and the blood began to flow, establishing the most basic of connections between them. He knew her vampire mojo was working on him as his body shivered in an echo of the ecstasy he'd felt in her arms. Bloodletters had a way of bringing pleasure even as they drained their prey of precious blood—the life force that sustained them.

His cock rubbed against her soft body, the layer of cloth between them the only barrier. He would remain clothed. He wouldn't force himself on her. Not even with her magic making him hard. She'd walked away from him once. He wouldn't do anything to make her do so again.

This time, he wanted to woo her into staying with him. For the moment, she was too weak to go anywhere, but he knew it wouldn't be smart to press his advantage. If he made love to her again, it had to be by her choice. And he knew he had to move slowly. He didn't want to scare her off again.

As near as he could figure, the intensity between them the last time they'd come together had scared her as much as it had him. While he'd been ready to embrace the change—given a little bit of time to think about it—she had fled. He wouldn't let that happen again. Or, at least, he'd give it his best shot. He couldn't make her stay if she didn't want to. If he tried, he'd be as bad as the bastard who had kept her prisoner. He would never clip her wings. Never cage her emotionally or physically. If she stayed—and he was going to do everything in his power to make that happen—it would be because she loved him as much as he loved her.

He felt almost giddy as she drank more deeply this time. Her body gained strength even as he held her under the warm mist of the shower. And he knew she felt the same pleasure he did as she writhed against him. He couldn't help the slight pulse of his thighs that rubbed his hard cock up against her.

It was impossible to stop the attraction, especially with the vampire magic doing a number on his libido.

Mag grit his teeth and tried to hold off the climax that built with every suck of her mouth against his neck, every rub of her nearly bare body against his fully clothed form. She rubbed her hips against him, their heights a perfect match for ultimate pleasure. And when he couldn't hold back any longer, he came in his pants with a groan of surrender.

She squirmed a bit more and then shuddered as her teeth bit down even harder for a long moment, her body spasming against him as she found completion as well. He held her tight, anchoring her to him while the warm water encased them in a mist—the two of them together, with no one else in the entire world. Just them. And their mutual pleasure.

At length, as her body quieted, her teeth retracted from his skin and the pressure of her bite eased. She licked him gently as he felt a tiny bit of magic seal the wounds. He'd wear her mark for a while—that had been one hell of a love bite, and she had more strength than the average female—but he didn't mind at all. In fact, he almost wished his shifter constitution wouldn't make the mark of her possession disappear too fast. He healed quickly, but he wanted to be able to look in the mirror and see that this hadn't been just another dream.

Having her in his arms, in his house, was every dream he'd ever had since that night they'd been together. The pleasure he felt with Miranda was unlike any other. His heart had opened up that night more than two years ago, and she had taken up residence there, never to be ousted. For the first time in his life, Mag could say he was truly in love.

Only, for the past two years, the love had been tinged with heartbreak. She'd left him and his inner cat had barely survived the blow. He hadn't spent much time in his fur since that night. The cat was too depressed. It didn't understand the nuances the human side of him grasped. It didn't understand that his mate was a vampire and was therefore off-limits. The cat only knew what it wanted. What it needed.

Miranda. Always Miranda. Forever Miranda.

And the cat was downright depressed without her. When Mag shifted into his cat form, that depression was harder to bear. But now the cat was happy again. Mag could feel it as easily as he felt the man's satisfaction of having Miranda in his home.

"Are you all right?" Her whisper caught him off guard. He'd been waxing philosophical, while they both recovered from an intense orgasm.

"Never better," he quipped and meant it. He'd never felt better than when he had her in his arms.

"I'm sorry. I didn't want to hurt you."

"Hurt me?" He had to laugh. "Honey, that was about as far from hurting me as you can get. Thank you."

She pulled away and looked up into his eyes. She seemed confused and he couldn't resist leaning down and placing a playful kiss on the tip of her nose.

"You're thanking me for biting you so hard, I left a mark?" Her gaze leapt to his neck, her eyes widening as she took in the bruising he knew had to be around the wound. He didn't mind it, but she seemed horrified.

"Sweetheart..." He used his finger under her chin to guide her gaze back up to his. "I loved every minute of it and I love even more that you're not fainting on me and scaring me with your weakness. You have a little color in your cheeks, which gratifies me to no end, and in case you didn't notice, I came right before you did, so I don't mind one little bit. Bite me again." His smile dared her and he was glad to see he'd surprised her with his words.

The color in her cheeks deepened. Had he ever seen her blush before? It seemed this was a night of unusual moments. He hadn't come in his pants since he'd been a teenager and then he'd been embarrassed. Tonight he felt kind of noble for not taking advantage of her. And sticky. Yeah, he was beginning to feel a little sticky.

"Do you mind if I get clean? I promise no funny business. I'm here to take care of you, not the other way around. At least not until you're much, much healthier." He smiled at her, shooting her a mischievous wink. "And even then, it'll be your choice, Miranda. I want you to stay, but only if you want it too. For now, I just want you to focus on recovering from your ordeal. Consider my home a safe haven for you—for however long you need it."

"Why?" she whispered. "Why are you doing this for me?"

She seemed so confused, he had to lay his heart on the line.

"Because I love you. Whether it's right or wrong doesn't matter. My cat knew its mate the moment I scented you. You're the only woman I will ever love, Miranda. For me, there is no other."

CHAPTER THREE

He would have said more, but she reached up and covered his lips with her fingers. Pain filled her eyes as she gazed up at him.

"Don't say it. I can accept your hospitality. I don't have much choice at the moment." She looked pained to admit her weakness. "But I refuse to accept anything else. We are *not* mates. We can't be."

Her protestations sounded weak to him, as if she was trying to convince herself. For the first time in more than two years, Mag had hope. She did feel something but, as he'd both hoped and feared, she was running from it.

He kissed her fingers, then took her hand from his lips, twining their fingers together. He held her gaze and decided caution was the better part of valor.

"We don't have to think about any of that now. All you have to do is get better. You were as close to death as I've ever heard a bloodletter being. You've been systematically wounded over a period of time. You won't get healthy in a few hours or even a few days. This could take a while and I'll be here for you as long as it takes. Whatever happens after…well…that's in the hands of the Goddess. I'm leaving that up to Her for now."

Miranda looked skeptical, but she slowly nodded and he

let her go. She was strong enough to stand on her own and after a moment, she reached for the liquid soap he kept along the stone ledge of the giant shower stall. She moved away and began to clean herself.

He decided to do the same. He stripped off his wet clothes quickly and stepped toward the jets on his side of the long shower. There were spray jets all over the enclosure and rain heads above. He tinkered with the controls so that the jets nearest him were a little more forceful and started the rain falling over both of them in a gentle patter.

She looked up, seemingly enchanted by the rain head right above her. She looked over her shoulder to smile at him and he saw her eyes widen as she realized he was naked. He grinned and soaped up his chest, wishing her hands were rubbing over him, not his own. But they had time to work up to that. He would have to be patient.

She turned away and finished cleaning her body, though she still wore the lacy bra and panties. She stood directly under the rain head, facing away from him as she began to shampoo her hair. It was knotted in places and he knew she'd need some extra help with the tangles. He finished rinsing and stepped out of the shower to rummage under the sink on the other side of the room. He kept toiletries under there that he'd bought with her in mind a long time ago.

Finding what he wanted, he went back to the shower. She was just finishing rinsing the soap out of her hair when he reached around, putting the bottle he'd found into her hand.

"Conditioner might help," he offered, wondering what she'd make of his preparedness.

"You had this on hand?" She turned enough to look up into his eyes. Suspicion marred her expression.

"I bought it when I finished building this bathroom. It's never been used."

She looked down, examining the seal on the bottle and then looked back at him. "Why would you buy this if you don't use it?"

"I thought maybe…" How did he explain this without

scaring her off? He had to tread carefully, but he also couldn't lie to her. Lying wouldn't help anything. "I hoped maybe one day, you'd be here to use it. The scent reminded me of you."

She opened the bottle and lifted it to her nose. Vampires had senses that were almost as acute as shifter senses, so strong scents were out. All the toiletries and cleaning products in the house had gentle, natural scents and were usually made with organic products.

"Roses and cinnamon? It's very subtle, but smells wonderful."

"The ingredients include rose hips and an extract of cinnamon that is supposed to be good for your scalp," he added, feeling the need to justify his purchase of the conditioner he never used. "You smell of roses and cinnamon to me," he added, admitting the truth of why he'd really bought it.

"I do?" She seemed surprised. And pleased, if he was any judge. She even smiled before turning her back and opening the bottle. She put a handful of the conditioner on her wet hair and worked it through.

He wanted to help, but he figured he'd pushed her enough for one night. She was looking a little better thanks to his blood, but she was already beginning to lose some of that sparkle. She'd been tortured over a long period of time. She wouldn't get better in a few hours. He had to remember to take things slowly with her. She needed time to heal—and time to get used to the fact that he was in her life and he wouldn't be easily left behind this time.

He left her in the shower, keeping the door open as he went into the master suite to dress. He would be able to hear her if she needed him. Meanwhile, he gathered some sweats that would be very loose on her and one of his oldest, softest T-shirts. She'd be comfortable, though not exactly a fashion plate. Tomorrow, he'd get clothes for her, but for tonight, this would do.

He threw on a similar outfit and reentered the bathroom. She spun around, her fangs dropping as if she sensed a threat.

Immediately he went on guard, but he couldn't sense anything. As far as he knew, his house was secure and neither his state of the art alarm system nor his heightened shifter senses reported anything amiss.

"Miranda?" he asked cautiously. "What's wrong?"

Her gaze was confused as she clutched a towel to her breasts. She still wore the lacy underwear but she'd stepped out of the shower and had a towel wrapped around her hair in addition to the one she'd been using to dry herself.

Mag watched her eyes, noting the moment when the fear left them to be replaced by confusion. She looked at him, her fangs retracting as she appeared to come back to reality. He'd startled her and somehow sent her back to the months of captivity—or so he guessed. He could have kicked himself. Mag knew he had to be patient and here he was, barging into the bathroom as if he owned the place.

Well, he *did* own the place, but he knew what he'd meant. He should have knocked or at least said something before he just walked in. A bathroom wasn't a place where you expected a lot of through traffic. He shouldn't have scared her.

"I'm sorry. I didn't mean to startle you."

"Mag?" She sounded so lost, he couldn't help himself.

He stepped closer, moving slowly so as not to provoke another untoward response. When she didn't react, he placed the clothes he'd brought for her on the vanity and reached forward, tugging her into his arms. She didn't resist. In fact, she clung to him after only a moment's hesitation.

"It's okay, sweetheart. You're safe. Nothing can harm you here. I've got you." He murmured soothing words to her as he rocked them both back and forth. She was trembling with reaction and returning fatigue. She was in rough shape, and it was his duty—his honor—to protect her and care for her while she recovered.

When she felt a little steadier, he released her. Desert nights could get cold and he didn't want to be selfish. He was fully clothed while she was still standing there in soggy undies and a towel. He had to let her dress and get more comfortable so she could rest.

"It's getting late. Dawn will be here in a short while. Let's get you settled and you can rest easy for the day."

"Do you have a sealed room?" She rubbed her arm as he stepped back.

"Honey, the entire house has been light-proofed. Once the shades come down, they can't be raised until nightfall. It's all computer controlled and the moment we got here, I activated that mode for you. The bedroom is an interior room and is built with reinforced walls and doors. Once you go to sleep for the day, you'll be safe. And should anything happen, there's even a bolt hole accessible from the bedroom where you can hide. I'll give you the grand tour as soon as you're dressed."

He saw the questions in her eyes, but he left without waiting for her to ask them. He'd made a lot of admissions here tonight and they sat uncomfortably on his mind. So far, he'd been the one laying himself on the line. He shouldn't expect more from her. Not now. Especially not after she'd been through so much and hadn't had any time yet to heal from her ordeal, but something inside him wanted her to jump into his arms and admit her undying love all the same. It was unrealistic. Silly, even. But there it was.

Mag closed the bathroom door behind himself and waited on the other side. Eventually, he heard the soft swish of fabric from the other side of the door that told him she was getting dressed. Good. The sooner he showed her around and put her fears to rest, the sooner she could also rest. She'd need good, healing sleep—and a lot of it—before she'd be well again.

He moved away from the door toward the small wet bar he'd put in. It wasn't anything fancy. Just a small, well-stocked wine refrigerator and some crystal glasses on a side table. He took out the corkscrew and selected a bottle of California red that had been recommended by his brother Matt.

Matt knew more about vampires than anyone else Mag knew. Well…more than any other shifter, at least. Mag was acquainted with the local Master vampire, but he hadn't dared pose his questions about bloodletters to the Master. He hadn't wanted to raise suspicion.

It wasn't common for a shifter to be so inquisitive about vampire habits. In fact, it could be downright dangerous to show that kind of interest. The relations between shifters and bloodletters were better in this city than most, but it still wasn't done to be too nosey. And if Mag betrayed the real reason he was so interested, it could go badly. Miranda was still subject to the Master's rule and he could easily demand she leave Mag's house. That was something Mag didn't want to chance.

When the door to the bathroom clicked open, a waft of cinnamon and rose scent came toward him. It was followed a moment later by Miranda's hesitant steps. She was barefoot and holding a small bundle of damp fabric in her hands.

"Do you have a washer?" she asked tentatively.

"Yeah. I'll take care of those. I'll also get some new clothes for you today so you'll have something fresh to wear tonight."

"You're going out?" She seemed afraid all of a sudden and he realized he wouldn't be going anywhere. He'd have to call in some favors.

"I'm not going anywhere," he was quick to reassure her. "I won't leave the house. Not for one minute. I have some friends I can call on to help pick up a few things for you. Do you prefer any particular brands? I was thinking blue jeans. You look hot in jeans." He offered her a smile, hoping a little flirtation would take the fear out of her eyes.

"Jeans are fine, but can you trust these people? They're shifters, right? Won't they object to me being here?" She seemed weary, but definitely more alert than she had been before—especially if she was thinking that far ahead.

"I have a brother who is on friendly terms with a few bloodletters. He'll help, and he won't tell anyone that you're here. In fact…" Mag turned around to get the glasses of wine he'd poured from the table and held one out to her. "My little brother recommended this wine. He knows the vintner personally."

She accepted the glass and took a tentative sip, savoring the fine wine. "Maxwell Vineyards, right? Your brother knows Atticus Maxwell?"

"And his mate," Mag confirmed, taking a sip himself. The vintage was delicious. Maxwell really knew what he was doing. "They're acquaintances, but he seems closest to a guy he says used to be a British lord or something."

Silence stretched for a moment or two while they sipped their wine. He was doing his best not to scowl at the many wounds and burns still visible on her forearms, which were left bare by the T-shirt. Finally, she spoke softly into the quiet.

"I didn't know Maxwell had found his One." She seemed skeptical, but she sipped at the wine all the same.

"Apparently it happened a little while ago, but they're still in the honeymoon phase according to my brother." Mag reached behind himself to snag the bottle and refilled Miranda's glass. "Matt told me how wine affects bloodletters and why so many of the great vintners are vampires. He said something kind of poetic about how the fermented fruit of the vine was your last link to the sun and that it was a sort of distilled sunlight. He also said it helped you heal."

"He wasn't wrong," she admitted, drinking deeply. "I feel it bubble and pop inside my veins in a good way. Maxwell isn't one of the world's top wine makers for nothing. He's had centuries to perfect his craft. This is delicious as well as healing."

Mag put his glass aside and refilled hers before showing her around the master suite. "The controls for everything in the house are on the tablet on the bedside table. You can control everything from there and I've keyed in a code for you alone. The only other person with codes to this house is me. Nobody gets in or out without either you or I allowing it." He walked with her to the small nightstand and lifted the tablet. The screen blinked to life the moment he touched it.

"I didn't realize you were so high tech." She seemed impressed as she continued to sip at her wine.

"My brother Steve is the security expert in the family, but I learned a lot from him. I installed all this myself and it's top notch. I keep upgrading as new things come on the market." He spent the next few minutes showing her how to access the cameras located all around the property and how to lock down the master suite and the entire house. "And then there's this." He put down the pad and showed her a hidden doorway that led to the bolt hole he'd had built especially for her. "Press here and here, and when you hear the click..." He put actions to words and a hidden panel popped open. "Voila. Safe room. It's built like a vault. It's not on the electronic systems and I built it myself so nobody knows about it but me...and now you."

He led the way down the small staircase to the room he'd designed as a last defense should the house be breached. There was a bed, a bank of monitors that allowed anyone down here to see what was happening upstairs as long as the cameras had power, and a few medical supplies, but not much else. He'd built it with Miranda in mind and she didn't need food. He'd put a few cases of wine down here for storage, which she could also use. Basically the place was a hideout she could stay in until the sun set if she was attacked in the house during the day.

She looked it over and seemed impressed. "You've thought of pretty much everything."

"I've had a lot of time to plan," he admitted.

"When did you start building all of this?"

"I started planning the day you left. The actual building commenced about a week later." Silence greeted his admission and he counseled himself to be patient. Rome wasn't built in a day. He had to ease up and give her a little time and space to heal, but he couldn't avoid direct questions.

He ushered her up the stairs and motioned her toward the

bed. "You need to rest, sweetheart. The sun will be up shortly and I want you to feel safe. You're in control of the locks here." He moved in to place a kiss on her forehead. "You'll never be caged again, Miranda. Not if I have anything to say about it."

She felt so right in his arms. He stood, just holding her for a long, long moment. If the world ended right now, it would be all right. He had the woman he loved in his arms and all was right with his world. For just this one moment out of time.

Eventually though, he had to let her go. She swayed in his arms as the wine relaxed her. At least bloodletters had that much in common with other beings.

"Let's put you to bed. I'll take care of everything today and then tonight, when you wake, you'll have new clothes to put on and we can see about getting you well. Do you need another hit of blood before you go to sleep?" He held her away from him and watched her eyes closely. They were at half-mast as the wine took effect, but her color was good and she smiled slightly.

"No. I'm good for now. Mag, I can't thank you enough for all you've done to help me. I'm so glad you were there. I'm thankful it was you who got me out of that hellhole. If you hadn't been there, I know I'd probably be gone by now. I wasn't rational. I'm very much afraid that I'm still not completely rational, so for your own safety, lock down the suite and be careful when I wake tonight. I don't trust myself not to attack first and ask questions later."

He smiled at her, knowing that she was showing every sign of recovery if she was worried about those around her. The Miranda he knew cared more for others than she did herself. It was a good sign.

"I'll announce myself before I come in. I'm sorry about before with the bathroom. I should've knocked." He smoothed his palms down from her shoulders as he stepped back. He then leaned down to lower the blanket so she could slide into the bed.

She smiled at his actions. "Are you going to tuck me in? For real?"

He nodded solemnly, though his smile joined hers. "For real. You're in my care now, and I'm going to see to your every comfort."

Shaking her head, she nonetheless climbed into the bed, a bemused smile on her lips.

He tucked the blankets around her, enjoying the simple, caring act. This time, he knew she'd be there all day. And he would make sure he was with her when she woke. He wanted his to be the first face she saw upon waking this night and every night to come—if he could swing it.

It all started here and now.

He kissed her soundly as she settled back on the bed, her eyes closing as the sun rose outside the sun-proofed house. When he drew back, she was already asleep, in the deep sleep of her people. Weakened as she was from her ordeal, she wouldn't wake until the sun left the sky that night.

Mag looked at her for long moments, brushing her hair back from her lovely face. She really was here, in his house. Wonder of wonders. He sent a little prayer up to the Mother of All, thanking Her for interceding for them. For allowing Mag to be there, just when Miranda needed him most. For letting him be there to save her life. Mag didn't think he was too far off the mark believing that the Goddess had something to do with that amazing timing. He didn't believe in coincidences. Everything happened for a reason and he had to believe that the Lady was smiling on them.

He finally made himself leave the room, being certain to lock everything down so Miranda would be safe during the day. He'd installed the best and most technologically advanced in security measures with just this duty in mind. She would come to no harm during the day while she rested. He was as certain as he could be of it.

Closing and arming the door behind himself, Mag set out to start his day. He hadn't had any sleep, but shifters didn't need much. He had a lot of work to do today before he could rest. He'd grab a few hours of sleep this afternoon, after he'd set the wheels in motion.

For one thing, he had to order up some clothes in Miranda's size and he didn't want to leave that task to someone else. Silly as it was, he wanted to pick out the fabric she would wear next to her skin and the colors that would best compliment her rare beauty. He had to go shopping—online, of course.

He also needed to eat. A few steaks ought to do it. He needed to keep himself in top shape if he was going to be donating blood on a regular basis—and he really hoped he was. He also needed to arrange time off from the family business.

Redstone Construction could get along without him for a little while. Luckily, he'd just completed a project in the city and he wasn't due to start another for a few weeks. He could easily turn over that project to someone else without affecting the schedule. He had a few favors to call in. And lastly, he had to at least tell his eldest brother, Grif, that he would be out of touch for a while.

He knew Grif wouldn't approve of Miranda being anywhere near the Clan or even near Mag, but while Mag respected Grif's right to decide what was best for the Clan, Mag had long been his own man. He wouldn't give up Miranda again—even if it caused a rift with his family and his people. She was more important to him than any of those things, which was really saying something. Until he'd met her, Mag would've said there was nothing and no one who could come between him and his brothers. And then Miranda happened.

In one night, she'd become his world.

He went through the house and into his office, which was filled with high-tech computer equipment. From here, he could monitor the house and the surrounding desert as well as do any sort of work he needed to accomplish. He wouldn't leave the house. He refused to leave Miranda alone while she was so vulnerable. But he was going shopping.

The internet was his store and he'd have everything delivered to Matt. His little brother could be trusted to help and not pass judgment. Matt liked vamps. He might not go so far as to approve of Mag mating with one, but Matt had always had a good heart, and he'd definitely help Mag take care of Miranda. Mag fired up the computers and settled in to select only the best for his girl.

Silks, cashmere for the chilly desert night and some good, old fashioned jeans were the first order of business. He knew Miranda liked denim and she looked amazing in it. When he'd first seen her, she'd been wearing a pair of tight blue jeans that nearly made him choke. She was hot and he wanted to see her looking that good once again.

For comfort, he also threw in some super soft lounge pants in a silk blend that would stretch and move with her. Matching tops and some little sweaters so she wouldn't catch a chill. Mag had never liked shopping before, but he found he enjoyed picturing Miranda in the different outfits he selected from an exclusive boutique downtown that catered to the jet set. Nothing was too expensive for his mate.

Before he knew it, a couple of hours had passed and it was a decent time to start making calls. He first arranged for all the stuff he'd ordered online to be delivered to Matt. Then he called in a few favors with members of his construction team. He got one of the other guys to cover for him and arranged for time off. Then he had to call Grif.

He wasn't exactly looking forward to the censure he was more or less certain he'd hear in his older brother's voice. But when he rang the house, it was Steve who picked up the phone, his second eldest brother and the second in command of the Clan. If Steve was answering Grif's phone, it meant Grif was busy. Mag almost breathed a sigh of relief.

"Hey Steve." Mag started off slow, wanting to gauge his brother's mood before he launched into anything. He didn't want to fight with his family, though he sensed it was going to be inevitable at some point, if Miranda stayed.

"Mag! Where the hell have you been? What happened with

the vamp?" Steve sounded both angry and anxious. Not a good combination.

"Miranda is with me. She's in pretty bad shape. I'm going to help her." Mag laid it out there and let the chips fall where they may.

"Where are you? You're not in the Clan neighborhood. I checked." Steve sounded suspicious.

"I'm at my place in the desert. Don't track me down, bro. I need time."

"With the vamp? Why? What is she to you?"

Oh, man, now Steve sounded peeved. Mag didn't like dealing with Steve when he got pissy. Ex-Special Forces, Steve usually tried to beat the shit out of Mag when he was in this kind of mood and though Mag held his own, he usually ended up bruised and equally pissed off by the end of it.

"She's everything," Mag whispered, unable to lie.

"Shit." Steve's curse held no heat and remarkably, he backed off. "All right. Take your time. Get your head on straight," he advised. "Don't do anything hasty and call me if you need me. Anytime. Day or night. I've got your back, bro."

Mag was impressed and a little shocked, though he knew his brothers were always behind him. They were family. But he'd expected more of an argument. Instead, Steve was giving him room…and compassion. Who'da thunk it?

"Thanks, man."

"No sweat. And Mag? Be careful."

"Don't worry, I will."

Mag knew Steve meant for him to be careful of the vampire—and Mag would. He'd be so careful of her, she would never leave him again. He wanted her for keeps and he was going to do everything in his power to convince her that they were meant to be together. For always.

The hard part over, Mag placed his next call to Matt. He had to get his little brother to play delivery boy and he also had to find out more about Matt's vamp connections. Mag needed advice from an expert on how best to help Miranda recover.

CHAPTER FOUR

At dusk, Miranda woke in a strange place. Was she dreaming again? Would the soft bed and spacious room turn back into the filthy cage she'd been kept in for more days than she could count? That had happened too many times. Each time, more heartbreaking than the last.

But something was different. There was something warm in the dream bed with her. Scratch that. It was some*one* warm. She could hear his heart beating and the blood flowing through his veins. She could smell the fascinating scent that she associated with only one person—Magnus.

Miranda slowly turned her head, not daring to breathe lest she ruin the amazing dream she was having.

"Hey, gorgeous." Her dream spoke.

Magnus Redstone—the only man to ever stir her cold heart—was leaning on one elbow, his long legs stretched out on the other side of the wide bed. He was fully dressed, which seemed odd for a dream. Whenever she'd dreamed of him in the past, he'd been decidedly naked. His golden skin had gleamed in candlelight in her favorite fantasy.

But he was wearing faded jeans and a white T-shirt. He looked comfortable…and good enough to eat. Immediately her hunger rose and her fangs descended. She turned more fully toward him and he held up a hand. Between them was a wine glass full of red liquid.

Suddenly she remembered the night before and the Maxwell Vineyards vintage she'd consumed that had tasted so amazingly delicious. This wasn't a dream. She really was in Mag's bedroom at his place out in the desert, in his bed.

She sat up so fast, her head spun. Miranda took a moment to just breathe and take it all in.

She felt the bed move behind her as Mag's heat surrounded her from the back. He brought his arm around her, his hand still holding the glass.

"Drink this. It'll make you feel better."

Miranda took the glass and held it up toward her mouth, inhaling. It wasn't just wine.

She looked over her shoulder at him. "Blood?"

"I made a few calls. My little brother's friends were very helpful."

"You said your brother Matt knew Atticus Maxwell."

"You remember that from last night. Good." He seemed pleased and she realized he had indeed studied up on what blood deprivation did to her kind.

Memory loss was one of the symptoms, as were killing rage and insanity. She didn't feel crazy, but she definitely had gaps in her memory. Big, huge gaps that, on reflection, she was probably better off not remembering. She didn't really want to remember all those endless nights spent as a captive of the evil mage.

"Matt is acquainted with Maxwell, but he's on much more friendly terms with a guy named Sebastian. After some convincing and a little bit of arm-twisting, Matt put me in touch with him. Sebastian gave me some advice on how to help you. He also told me how to get hold of human blood supplies without raising too many eyebrows. Very helpful guy, is Sebastian. Drink up. There's more and it's as fresh as I could manage. It might not taste as good as right out of the vein, but my source says that mixing it with wine helps it taste better and it'll help you heal."

Still holding his gaze, she took a sip. He was right. It

wasn't as good as when she drank from a live being, but after having been mostly starved for who knew how long, it tasted fantastic. And it didn't have the magical zing of shifter blood that was hard for her to process in her weakened state. Mag's blood had saved her life last night, but she was too worn down to accept such richness as a steady diet right now.

Besides, it was an unwritten rule that vamps didn't dine on *weres*. For one thing, shifters didn't usually volunteer, and older vampires didn't like it when one of the younger generation jumped up in power quickly. A young vamp with a magical blood supply might possibly overpower an older, more experienced bloodletter and that wasn't to be tolerated. Their society relied on the hierarchy, and the hierarchy was decided by individual strength.

Since strength usually came with age, the older and more powerful vamps tended to rule over the younger and less experienced. If a youngster gained what was considered an unfair advantage by drinking magical blood on a constant basis, it was viewed as a cheat—though the cheater could be too strong to challenge outright. Such situations caused chaos, and chaos was to be avoided.

"Much as I would've liked to let you snack on me…" Mag continued as she sipped at the blood-laced wine, "…Sebastian said it would be better for you in the long run if you paced your recovery. I described your situation to him and he theorized that you were drained both physically and magically. You not only weren't fed the blood you need to survive, but you were bled as well. And along with your blood, the mage likely accessed your magic. All three things combined are some of the most serious problems a bloodletter can face. It didn't happen overnight, and you're not going to be back to one hundred percent health overnight either, I'm sorry to say. So we're starting you off with blood-laced wine. If you tolerate that well, in a month or so we can switch you to all blood and then when you're strong enough, you can go out and hunt some fresh human blood. I'll be with you through all of it, Miranda." His arms came around her from behind as his mouth nuzzled under her ear. She felt the scrape of his teeth—sharper than a human's. The feel of it sent a little thrill down her spine. "I'm not letting you go again, sweetheart."

That sounded serious and it made her worry. Nothing had changed. A relationship between them was doomed. Both their peoples had prohibitions against such unions. They'd face condemnation from every side.

"Mag, I—"

He cut off her objection by turning her head and kissing her. It was a sweet kiss edged with passion. A little preview of the naughty pleasure she knew only he could bring her. She was about to surrender to him when he moved back.

He licked her lips as he raised his head, his gaze holding hers as he put a little bit of space between them. She knew the taste of the wine—and the blood—wouldn't bother him. He was a predator, after all. In his cougar form he hunted and ate raw meat. Blood was nothing new to a shifter.

"Let's take this one step at a time. We have time yet to figure out where this road leads. For now, just concentrate on healing. Sebastian warned me that you'll be sleeping a lot more than usual. He said once you get set on the wine-blood diet, you might only be awake a couple of hours each night as your body takes the time to rest and heal. So let's make the most of our time together each night, okay? I haven't seen you in two years. We have a lot of catching up to do." He smiled that golden-boy, charming smile of his. "And I can show you around my home and the desert, if you like. We're way out in the middle of nowhere, but it's really beautiful out there."

He made it sound so simple. Live for the moment. She'd never been very good at that, but she knew she had no choice. All she had with Mag was the moment. They would never be allowed to make a go of it as a couple. Their people would pull them apart. Either his or hers. It didn't matter. Neither group would be happy about their union. So unhappy, they'd never let it happen.

But for now, he was right. She was as weak as she'd ever been—even when she'd been fully human. She needed to heal and she had nowhere else to go. Nowhere safe, at any rate. She knew Mag would watch over her while she recuperated and she trusted him like no other. She trusted him with her life. He'd take care of her and somehow, someday, she'd make it up to him. She couldn't be his mate, but she could owe him a debt of honor. A life debt.

In fact, she owed such a debt to his whole family and a few others in their Clan. For it was his brothers and the Clan's trackers who had found her. Sure, they'd probably been there to stop the mage, but the effect was to save her life as well. Even after she'd attacked one of them.

No question about it, she owed every person who'd been there last night.

"I'd like to see the desert with you," she finally agreed. She could take this one night at a time. At the moment, she really didn't have much other choice.

But she'd be on her guard against any hint of permanency with Mag. Her heart was already broken by the impossibility of their mating. She wouldn't allow it to hurt any deeper, which meant she'd have to remain a little distant. She had to protect what little was left of her heart.

Mag showed her around his impressive home, but that was about all she could handle. As he'd predicted, she was only able to stay awake for a little over an hour that night. Just enough time to drink a few glasses of blood-laced wine and take a hot bath before being given the nickel tour of the rest of the luxurious house.

By the time he'd filled her in on the remainder of the security measures he'd installed, her eyes were beginning to drift closed. He noticed and cut short the tour, lifting her into his arms and carrying her back to the bedroom. Like the night before, he tucked her in with a chaste kiss and she didn't know anything more until the next sunset.

The nights passed like this for more than a month, at

Miranda's best guess. She seemed to lose track of time again, but this time it wasn't in fear of death, but due to the comfort of knowing she was safe. Mag would take care of her. She trusted him.

The fear ebbed and she was able to sleep. Really sleep, without the constant worry that she'd be tortured and vulnerable. It was deep, healing sleep that took both her days and most of her nights, but each night she was awake a little longer and felt a tiny bit better.

She felt the intrinsic magic in her soul returning a little at a time. Mag was great. He didn't push her into anything that made her uncomfortable. He didn't press her to take their relationship—such as it was—to the next level. In short, he was her friend.

Since that first night, he'd stayed by her side during her waking hours. A few times, she knew, he'd left the house to do things with and for his family. He'd told her when they'd found the evil woman who'd murdered his mother. She'd hugged him while he mourned for his mother, offering the support of a friend, the embrace and touch that shifters seemed to need more than other people.

The next day he told her he'd had to leave just after she'd fallen asleep to attend the shifter memorial service they'd finally been able to hold for his mother. The matriarch's body had been sent to the earth and stars by the Clan's priestess, letting his beloved mother finally move on to the next world. Miranda had seen the tears in his eyes as he talked about the ceremony, and she had reached out to hug him. It was the least she could do to comfort a man who was clearly in pain.

He'd confessed his deep grief over the loss of his mother and had told her about the woman she'd never met. They'd really talked that night, for the few hours she was able to stay awake. She'd gotten to know the caring soul that lived deep inside him in a much more intimate way, through his words and the emotion he could not hide at such a vulnerable moment.

The next night, after an initial caution on his part, they

both seemed to realize they were closer than they had been before. They'd both seen each other at vulnerable times now and they'd shared the burden, drawing them closer.

It was in that new intimacy, a few nights later, that he seemed to feel able to ask the questions she had known were coming, but still wasn't sure she could answer. He sat with her on the couch in the spacious living room of his house, before a lovely, dancing fire in the hearth. He had one arm around her shoulders and they both held glasses of wine. Hers had that little extra ingredient—the blood that was helping her heal, slowly but surely.

"The last thing I really remember that gives me some reference to time was delivering Christmas presents to some human friends that run a wine bar I used to frequent. I've done that every year since they opened. It's a good excuse for a party that allows me to spend a little time among my few mortal friends." Miranda paused to take a sip of the blood and wine mixture that helped her heal. "I think that was a few weeks before I was captured. I remember feeling very down. Cassie was being a bitch, as usual, and I hadn't been really on my game since...well...since meeting you, if you must know." She made the admission in as casual a voice as she could manage.

Mag stroked her hair with a light touch. "It's okay. I know what you mean. I felt the same." His whispered words touched her, but she still refused to admit to the connection between them.

"Well...it made me sloppy. I continued to hunt, because I must, but I wasn't as careful as I should be and one night, I picked the wrong place, and the wrong mortal. I should've stuck to places like Raintree's club where there is some protection, but I went to a mortal bar. A dangerous place. I think I was seeking out the danger because I had no real care left for my personal safety. I was drifting. At loose ends. And very unhappy." She sipped her wine. "Childish, I know. Self-destructive behavior that got me captured."

"What happened, sweetheart? How did you get caught?"

His gentle voice urged her to remember, and to reveal the depths of her stupidity.

"There's a biker bar out on the edge of town, near the interstate. JR's Roadhouse." She paused.

"I've heard of it. I've even been there once or twice," he admitted. "It's not the kind of place I'd expect to find a lady."

She laughed, but the sound held no mirth. "Yeah. Well. Do you know about the effect certain kinds of tainted blood has on bloodletters?" She was loathe to admit the vulnerabilities of her race to anyone, but she trusted Mag. Filling him in on these vampire secrets would help him understand.

"Tainted? You mean like diseased?" He seemed kind of appalled at the idea.

"No," she was quick to correct his assumption. "Tainted as in laced with foreign substances."

"Like alcohol? Drugs?" The concept seemed to click for him.

"As you see, I can drink alcohol straight up. Wine is preferred, but anything with alcohol in it is pretty well tolerated by most bloodletters. That's about all we can ingest without paying a penalty of severe discomfort. "But when we drink human blood that has been tainted with certain drugs, well, the effect can carry over sometimes."

"Let me guess. We're not talking about synthetic compounds here, right? So...opiates, pot, things derived from plants?"

"You're quick." She raised her glass to him, nodding. "That bar is a distribution point. More than a few of those bikers were high. I was targeting them."

Mag's arm tightened around her shoulders as he squeezed her to his side. "I'm sorry."

"Sorry?" She turned a little to look at him. "Why should you be sorry?"

"Because in a way, I did that to you. If you hadn't met me and been in such a state—"

She placed one finger across his lips, stopping his words.

"Things happen as the Lady wills it. I've had enough time to contemplate my capture while I was being held and in the weeks since. I don't think there's anything anyone could've done to change what happened. As it turns out, while I was stalking the druggies, that mage was stalking me. He'd been on my trail for some time, apparently. Months. Years, maybe. He was just waiting for me to make a mistake, and boy did I make a mistake that night." She turned away from him, unable to finish her story while maintaining eye contact. "I chose a biker and took him outside. The parking area is dark and not safe at all. I thought I'd be okay with my immortal strength and speed and all, but after I drank from the guy, I was almost as impaired as he was. The drugs hit me along with the bloodrush and I staggered away…right into the trap the mage had set."

She stopped talking and swallowed hard, remembering those panic-inducing few minutes. She'd been unsteady on her feet, a little stoned, and oh-so-vulnerable. And then the mage had pounced.

"He had a silver net and silver cuffs. His magic negated my own in a way I'd never experienced before. He had been preparing his spells for a long time and when he sprang his trap, I was a goner. He knocked me out and I woke up in the cage." She was breathing hard, trying to hold back the sobs. She was afraid if she started to cry, she might never stop.

Mag turned her in his arms and hugged her close. She let herself lean on him for just a little while. He was so strong. So good and true. She'd been alone and adrift for so very long. He was her safe harbor. The light that led her home, to safe shores.

"Ssh. It's okay. You're safe now and he can never hurt you again." Mag rocked her in his arms.

"Thanks to you, Mag," she whispered. "I can never thank you enough for saving me. I was so near the edge. I don't think anybody else could have kept me from going over," she admitted. It was a hard admission to make, but she needed to speak the truth to him, of all people. "I can't even really say for sure how long he held me captive." She tried to shake off the threatening tears by pulling back, away from Mag, and changing the subject. "I remember Christmas, but that was a while before I was captured. And then, while he had me, as I started to fade, time took on a sort of hazy quality. I know it had to be at least eight-to-twelve months, maybe more, but I can't say for sure. After the first few weeks, I was too weak to really differentiate one night from the next."

Admitting that was painful. Even before she'd been captured, her use of drugged mortal blood had grown more frequent to the point where she didn't even know how long it had been since that Christmas party at the bar to the time she'd been captured. She'd been floating along, mortally wounded by finding, then losing, her One. She hadn't cared about much of anything and had been merely surviving from one night to the next. She hadn't really been living. Not since she'd left Mag's bed an hour before dawn after that single night they'd spent together.

Since then, her life had been empty. Almost not worth living. And then she'd been captured and it had only gotten worse. She shuddered, thinking about it, and Mag's arm came back around her shoulders.

"I'm so sorry, Miranda," he whispered. "I'm sorry you had to go through all that."

She nodded, not looking at him. The dancing flames in the fireplace helped her focus. She watched them.

"It's okay. Maybe my mother was right, and things really do happen for a reason. If that particular mage hadn't caught me then I probably would never have seen you again. And with the way I was going, I probably would have died already. I wasn't really thinking all that clearly right before I was captured. If it hadn't been that mage, it could just as easily have been one of my rivals, or even those mortal bikers I preyed on. One of them might've gotten lucky and hurt me enough to end my existence. Who knows? I was playing Russian roulette with the way I was behaving. Something would've gotten me if the mage hadn't."

It was only the truth, but she felt really bad admitting it. Still, perhaps coming clean with her troubles was a first step to overcoming them. Mag had been more like a psychotherapist than a potential lover lately, and he'd already proven himself to be a good friend.

Mag cared for her in the truest sense of the word, and his gentle actions meant the world to her. She was so weak. She couldn't have handled any pressure from him to commit to a romantic relationship. If he'd pressured her, she would have left—no matter how weak she was. She would have walked out into the desert and done her best to find shelter before the sun rose…but if she hadn't been able to, she would have met her fate.

She would have died the final death.

It had been so close to her now for so long. Each night she had woken in the mage's cursed silver cage, she'd thought the final death would be her reward. But the bastard had kept her on the very edge of life for months, maybe longer. He had seemed to enjoy her misery. It had felt as if he *wanted* to push her over the edge into insanity. She remembered how he'd rejoiced when she ranted and pushed herself against the silver bars that were corrosive to her flesh, trying to get her hands on him. He'd enjoyed watching her suffer.

But thanks to Mag and his family, that was all over. Mag watched over her recovery with an intensity that made her feel cherished and special. And he never asked for anything in return. All he seemed to want was her welfare.

Though she knew, in both of their hearts, they wanted more. Mag was just more open about it. He touched her with affection when he held her hand or steadied her trembling body. He kissed her at least once each night, sometimes more. She allowed it because she was powerless to resist his gentleness. He was such a good man. A brave soul, who had stepped in during her darkest moment to save her, when everyone else saw her for the ravening beast who could have easily killed them all.

She would never forget that. Never be able to thank him

enough—for saving her that night, and for his gentleness on all the nights since as he watched over her recovery. Little by little, the amount of blood mixed with Maxwell's healing vintages increased until she was able to drink human blood almost straight.

She had lost track of time again. When she'd been a prisoner, she'd wandered into a hazy world where she had no real knowledge of the passage of time. Now, in her recovery, she was doing the same. Only before, it had been a way of protecting herself from the knowledge that she had been a captive for far too long. Now, it was due to comfort.

Mag kept her so comfortable, she didn't really worry when one night blended into the next. It was all good, and her every need was met by Mag's quiet, thoughtful ways. He'd given her beautiful, soft, expensive clothing—every piece a perfect fit. He'd gone to the trouble of finding the best way to help her heal. He'd been nothing but kind to her and each night they sat talking for longer and longer every time.

He helped her mind heal until she was no longer worried she might snap at any moment and savage him. No, the only real fear she had now was that she'd jump his bones.

Vampires fed on sex and blood. She was working her way up to fresh human blood again—in fact she was almost ready to go out and hunt. And when she did, she'd make her prey come. The blood was always sweeter and more potent at the moment of climax. She'd feed on her prey's blood and the intoxicating energy of their orgasm.

She hadn't had actual sex with anyone since Mag. In truth, she hadn't had sex with anyone for a long time before him either. He was special. Tempting. Addictive.

Forbidden.

She wouldn't have sex with her human prey, but she'd make them come. It was the least she could do to leave her victims with a pleasant, if hazy, memory of getting off with a pretty girl. That way they both benefitted, and it made her feel better about taking their blood without their conscious knowledge.

She'd been able to manipulate mortal memories since almost the very beginning. It was a basic skill all vamps acquired and used to maintain secrecy. Most mortal minds were incredibly susceptible to her magic, but not shifters. And especially not Magnus Redstone.

He'd impressed her from the very beginning. The moment she'd spotted him—or rather, that he had spotted her working her magic on a mortal and made his presence known—she'd known he was different. He'd come over and subtly warned her off the prey she'd chosen that night in a random bar in Las Vegas. The mortal had been a friend of Mag's and he had made it clear in unspoken ways that the man was under his protection.

Then later that night, after they'd gotten to know each other a bit, Mag had made it clear that he'd allow her a taste of his powerful shifter blood in return for a night in her bed. She'd been sorely tempted. An offer of shifter blood was too good to turn down. She'd gone with him to a luxury hotel room on the Las Vegas Strip and spent the night having the best sex of her life and a delicious taste of forbidden shifter blood. The combination had sent her into orbit.

Then she'd heard his thoughts as if they were her own and for a split second, the universe opened up before her. She knew she had found her One.

But it couldn't be. He was a shifter.

She'd ruthlessly slammed the barriers down between her mind and his, and though he'd looked at her quizzically, she'd quickly realized he hadn't really understood what had happened. Shifters didn't normally share their minds with anyone. That wasn't the way they mated. But for bloodletters, the sharing of thoughts, of memories, of souls…that was what every vampire dreamed of finding, just once in their immortal lifetimes.

And she'd found that with Mag. A shifter. Someone she could never have.

"Maybe tomorrow we can go into town and try a little hunting," Mag said conversationally as he sat down next to her in the library. It had become her favorite room in the house. It was filled with a rather impressive antique book collection and the fireplace was cozy during the cool desert nights. "But before we do, there's something we need to take care of."

She looked up at him when he knelt beside her wing chair. There were two comfy, old leather wing chairs placed in front of the fire—one on either side. She'd claimed the one on the right and he always sat on the left when they shared quiet hours and bottles of wine in this room. But he'd changed things up, kneeling before her, a basin and cloth in one hand.

"What's that?" She was intrigued by the serious look on his face.

"An experiment of sorts, though Matt's vampire friend swears it should work now that your strength is returning. You see..." he took her left arm in his hands and gently tugged it toward him. "It pains me to see these scars on your skin. The cuts sealed and stopped bleeding that first night, but they've left marks. And the burns are still discolored. Without treatment, Sebastian says they could take months to fade. So he suggested this."

"What did he suggest exactly?" She didn't like him drawing attention to the visible reminders of her ordeal. She hated looking at them and spent as little time examining her damaged skin as possible. Vampires didn't have scars. At least, they shouldn't, in the normal course of business.

"A wine bath. Apparently, the wine should react with your skin to help decrease the visibility of the marks."

"You're going to waste a perfectly acceptable—and expensive—bottle of wine on my skin?"

"Absolutely. If it restores you to health, I will do just about anything. Haven't you realized that by now, sweetheart?"

The look in his eyes nearly melted her heart, but she couldn't let it affect her. They were not meant to be. There were too many prohibitions against a union like theirs, especially considering she was very young for a vampire. The older ones would be furious if they ever realized she'd fed from a shifter even once. The boost in power just from a few sips was an unacceptable jump up for someone so young and new to immortality.

When she didn't reply, Mag sighed and reached for the bottle of wine he'd left on the floor near her chair earlier. It was already open. All he had to do was pull out the cork and pour the wine into the crystal bowl he'd brought. There was a small sea sponge already in the bowl and it quickly absorbed the costly vintage.

She let him do as he liked, allowing him to place the wide bowl on her lap and stretch her forearm across it. He used gentle strokes with the saturated sea sponge, tracing the path of every scar and burn mark on her arm. She watched, wondering if it really would work. She'd never tried such a thing before, though she was well aware of the benefits of drinking wine, she hadn't tried it externally.

To her amazement, the wine began to bubble and tingle against her skin. When the sensation stopped and Mag retraced the area with the sponge, the marks looked visibly lessened. For the first time in a long time, Miranda smiled.

"I think it's working."

"Yeah, it's definitely working," he agreed. "Not as fast as I'd like, but it looks better already. If we do this each night for a while, you might be back to your unblemished state in no time."

The very next night, Mag took her out of the house in a sedate, very expensive, silver Mercedes. The luxury car rode like a dream through the desert night. Dusk was gone and true night had fallen before they'd left the house way out in the desert. He'd driven for a little over an hour before the lights of Las Vegas came into view.

He'd been pointing out landmarks along their route so she'd know how to get back to the house. She'd also been watching the roads they'd taken and had committed them to memory. She was confident she could find his oasis in the desert now from wherever she ended up.

"Do you have a preference of hunting grounds?" Mag surprised her by asking. Or at least, the way he phrased the question surprised her. Then again, he was also a predator. He understood the hunt. That was just another reason she felt so comfortable with him, she supposed.

"Have you heard of Raintree's? It's a dance club and bar downtown. Do you know it?"

Mag nodded, a slight growl in his voice when he answered in the affirmative. It was almost as if he was angry, but repressing his instincts to scratch and claw. She didn't really understand where that reaction was coming from, but she was instinctively cautious.

"Are you sure about this?" Mag asked her as they drove through the outskirts of the city.

"I know my duty." If she was going to feed from human prey, she had to follow certain procedures. Her choice of destination was part of that. She was taking a bit of a chance, but she had to be brave. Defying the Master's will wasn't something she could get away with. She wasn't nearly strong enough or highly-placed enough in the bloodletter hierarchy to even think about it.

As they neared their destination and she began to pick up on the energy and scent of the mortals all around them, her instincts went on high alert. Her hunger was driving her now and she needed desperately to feed. She didn't entirely trust herself to stop at just a sip, so in a way, she was grateful for Mag's presence. She knew he could handle whatever she could dish out, and he'd stop her from hurting anyone in her bloodlust. It was reassuring to know—for the first time in years—that someone truly had her back.

He pulled up in front of the somewhat exclusive club and let the valet take his car while he ushered her into the intimate grip of the dance and drinking establishment that catered to a higher class of visitor to the Las Vegas scene. High rollers had made this place their hangout. After a big win, many rich tourists could be found here, drinking expensive champagne and throwing about their winnings like so much play money. The wait staff was top notch and often went home with ridiculous tips for good service. Hundred dollar bills were just the tip of the iceberg and the owner of this place could pick and choose the best and most beautiful workers to populate his domain.

The owner, of course, was immortal.

CHAPTER FIVE

Raintree was the Master's right-hand man. Checking in with him before hunting in his domain was considered a courtesy and would be almost as good as going straight to the Master. By seeking out Raintree with Mag in tow, she was taking a bit of a chance, but Miranda had to let the Master's people know what had happened to her.

Entering the dark atmosphere of the busy club, Miranda didn't even pause by the bar area. Instead, she went straight to the rear of the building and up a flight of well-concealed stairs. Mag followed her every move. A vampire waited at the top, blocking her way.

She knew who he was, even though she had never had direct dealings with him. His name was Boris and he was only a few years older than her. He was reputed to have been a Chicago gangster in the 1920's before he'd been transformed, but his character hadn't changed much. He worked for Raintree as a bully boy. A thug.

"Why did you bring the dog?" Boris's tone was insulting.

"I'm a cat, actually." Mag's flippant observation wasn't helping the situation.

Miranda stepped in. "I owe him a life-debt."

That should have been enough to grant them passage, but the guard seemed unimpressed. She tried again.

"I have been held captive by a *Venifucus* mage for almost a year and not one of my own kind even thought to look for me." She knew her voice held more than a bit of her contempt and hurt, and that seemed to get through to Boris at last. His façade slipped a bit. "This man saved me. He found me, nursed me back to the state I am in now and has done more for me than any of the Brotherhood ever has. I will not be parted from him, but I will follow rules and report my presence to Raintree. Either summon him or get out of my way."

Where she found the backbone to stand up to big, bad Boris, she didn't know. Although she had to admit, the two-hundred pound shifter at her back seemed to lend her strength. The low growl he kept trying to suppress as his anger rose fed her own indignation as well. They were both pissed and now Boris knew it.

"Wait here." Boris stepped away, leaving two of the regular—mortal—security team in his place.

The guards effectively blocked the way to the upper floor, leaving Mag and Miranda exposed on the upper steps. She watched Boris go down the hall, into a room she knew from prior experience was Raintree's front office. A moment later he stepped back out again and crooked his finger. The mortal guards stepped back, allowing Miranda and Mag to finish the climb to the second floor.

Mag was right behind her as Miranda walked toward the office door. Boris stood back, allowing them to enter, then closed the door behind them. They were in the outer sanctum—Raintree's public office. She knew his inner sanctum had to be much better hidden, and he didn't allow anyone but the most trusted of his associates into that area. Miranda had never been there and didn't care to vie for that dubious honor. She had always been happier being her own woman, and hadn't ever sought the protection of an older companion among the other immortals. Maybe that was why she'd been such easy pickings for the evil mage, but Miranda wouldn't change her core principles. Not now. Not ever.

"Ah. Little Miranda. I'd wondered what happened to you." Raintree didn't bother to stand from behind his enormous desk. He merely smiled a toothy smile, allowing his fangs to show, and motioned for them to sit in the antique chairs set up in front of the mahogany desk. Like children being called before a very elegant principle.

"Apparently you didn't wonder enough to bother looking for me," she muttered. She would not be cowed by this man. She'd been timid before, but after her ordeal, she would never kowtow to anyone ever again.

Raintree seemed taken aback for an instant, but he hid his response almost immediately. Good, she thought. Let him realize I'm different now. Experience tempers a person.

"What brings you to my door? Aside from the obvious, of course." Raintree was smooth. She'd give him that. "And who is your very interesting companion?" He turned his head just fractionally toward Mag.

"Magnus Redstone, this is Aramis Raintree, second only to the Master of Las Vegas."

"Redstone?" Finally, Raintree deemed Mag worthy of his attention. "One of the five brothers, I presume. The Master speaks well of the eldest, Griffon."

"I'm the middle brother," Mag answered politely, but said nothing more. Good, Miranda thought. Let Raintree work for whatever information he got.

"And how do you know our Miranda?" Raintree asked, looking only slightly pained at having to make small talk with a shifter.

"We are old acquaintances," Mag replied with a somewhat vague wave of one hand. Miranda loved the byplay. Much was being said here, without words. It was the power struggle between shifter and vamp that really held everyone's attention.

"She claims you saved her from a mage? Tell me, Miranda," Raintree shifted gears, seeming to realize that he would have to work harder for information from the cat. "What exactly happened to you?"

She'd known she would have to report the incident, but now that the moment was upon her, she was just tired of it all. Tired of the game playing. Tired of the posturing. Tired of the hierarchy and all their insidious rules. She sighed heavily before abbreviating her answer.

"I hunted in the wrong place and got caught in a trap. The mage caged me in silver and starved me for a long time, cutting me and taking my power. Mag and his family were hunting the mages that murdered their matriarch. The man who caged me was one of them. Mag found me, freed me, and he's been taking care of me while I regained enough strength to try hunting for myself. This is the first time I've been back to the city since I was captured. I came here to report in and do my duty. Apart from that, I wish only to feed and then leave once again. I request right of passage and license to hunt in your domain."

Raintree seemed nonplussed, as if he had expected a lot more detail and less backbone from someone her age. By vampire standards, she was very young and the elders always seemed to want to rub in how much she had yet to learn. But Raintree's gaze held nothing of the indulgent contempt she was used to from him. Rather, he seemed almost impressed. A new respect seemed to gleam from his dark eyes. It quickly turned to suspicion when he shifted his gaze to Mag.

"Are you feeding from him?" Raintree demanded bluntly. You know it cannot be allowed on a continuous basis. One hit might be overlooked. I mean, who hasn't wanted to walk on the wild side if given a chance? But the elders will not be pleased if you have reached some kind of arrangement between yourselves to try to enhance each other's power. That would be seen as cheating and could get you both sanctioned."

"Look at my neck, dickhead," Mag said quietly, stretching his chin upward and scratching with his middle finger. Crude, but funny. Miranda had to hold back a laugh. How Mag could be so calm while challenging one of the most powerful vampires in the city, she had no idea. The cat had balls. Big ones. "I gave her what she needed to live the night we rescued her, but it's been a strict diet of wine and small amounts of donated human blood ever since, just to get her strong enough to leave the house. She's been following all your stupid rules."

"How did you know what to give her?" Raintree's mask slipped yet again. He seemed both astonished and intrigued.

"My little brother has friends among the Napa Valley bloodletters. There's a guy named Sebastian who gave me some pointers. He said your Master was welcome to check with him, and he offered to vouch for my family. So did the Napa Master, Marc LaTour. Call them if you want confirmation."

"Rest assured, I shall." Raintree's speech slipped back into the patterns of days long past—a sure sign of stress. He seemed to catch himself and took a deep breath before continuing in a more businesslike tone. "I think the Master will want to talk with you both. Expect a summons. In the meantime, you have leave to hunt, Miranda, but all the usual rules apply. And under no circumstances are you to drink from your shifter host or offer him the benefit of your fluids. It is not allowed. You're lucky I can't demand you separate, but that is up to the Master."

Mag stood before she did. "Good," he said with a hearty smile that had to grate on Raintree's already stressed nerves. "Then we're done here?" Miranda had to stifle a giggle at the way Mag tempted the powerful vampire. The cat was pushing the big, bad Rottweiler, bopping him on the nose with a quick, furry paw.

"We're done. For now. Watch your step, cat. This is my domain and I don't really care who your brother is when you're in my establishment." Raintree stood as well, which was a clear sign Mag had rattled him. His pose of indulgent, almost insulting repose was well and truly shattered. Miranda rose gracefully from her chair and took Mag's arm.

"Thank you for your kindness, Aramis," Miranda said in a deceptively calm voice. She'd never dared call Raintree by his first name before, but it was her little way of standing in unity with Mag and confirming that she had changed. The other vamps had better watch out. She was about to move up in the hierarchy—whether they liked it or not.

One didn't survive the ordeal she had gone through without changing on a fundamental level. She had grown. She had come through it stronger. Mostly thanks to Mag. She owed him her allegiance. By contrast she owed her fellow immortals nothing. They would have let her die when Mag had done all he could to save her. That was something she would never forget. Not as long as she lived, which could be a very long time indeed.

"This isn't gonna work," Mag growled an hour later.

He'd watched while Miranda had selected a young, human male. She'd chatted him up at the bar and used her vamp mojo to get him out onto the dance floor. Then she'd taken him toward the back of the room where there were a few private alcoves in which the vamps could do their business with the mortals they preyed on.

Mag had bristled all the while, watching closely should Miranda need backup. The other bloodletters in the room gave him a wide berth and the bartender served him like he did all the humans. Apparently the barman didn't recognize a shifter when he saw one, though he was careful to give the vamps only the best wine, held in a separate cooler just for them.

Mag nursed his beer, sidling over to the back of the room so he could watch over Miranda and her mark. He wouldn't let her out of his sight. Not in a place like this. No matter what the bloodsucking twerp upstairs had said, Mag didn't trust any of the vamps here.

His inner cougar was clawing at him as he watched Miranda lead the young man to one of the dark alcoves. Humans couldn't see well in the dark. Not like vamps and shifters. To Mag, the darkened area was as clear as day. He moved closer. He would remain within leaping distance in case anything went wrong. Miranda was far from full strength. Even a human could overpower her in her current state.

But she needed fresh blood to continue healing. It irked him to no end. And it drove his cat to the point of insanity. His wild side didn't understand how he could just stand there and watch his mate making time with another guy. Touching a human. Leading him into a dark corner and…yes…she struck, biting him cleanly.

Mag wanted to growl and screech and drag the guy away from her, preferably breaking every bone in his miserable body along the way. But the rational side of him knew this was what she needed. He tried to be analytical as he watched her suck and swallow. Once. Twice. A third time. Mustn't be greedy. Don't leave the prey too weak to explain.

She looked up, her red-rimmed eyes meeting his and he watched her regain control. She moved back, licking the wounds on her mark's neck closed with a little zap of her vamp magic. Already she was stronger for having fresh, pure, human blood.

She dropped her prey to the chair behind them, setting him up with a fruity energy drink the vamps kept back there for exactly that purpose. He had a dreamy look in his eyes as he drank without even realizing what he was doing. No doubt, she'd left him with a pleasant memory of fucking some nameless, faceless girl in the back of the club. As far as the guy knew, he'd gotten lucky that night.

It was neatly done and Mag had to admire her skill as she walked toward him, a little more spring in her step than there had been since he'd rescued her. He'd hated every moment of watching her feed from some other guy, but seeing her returning strength made it all worth it.

She strode right up to his side and slid under his outstretched arm. He dropped his beer bottle on an empty table as they walked together out of the noisy club.

"This would be so much easier if you could just drink from me," Mag observed in a soft tone meant only for her to hear.

She drew back, her eyes widening in alarm as she looked over at him. "You know I can't. You heard Raintree. And he's just the tip of the iceberg. Your people wouldn't like it either."

Mag sighed as they exited the club and the valet ran to get his car. "I know, but my beast doesn't understand."

"You don't have to come with me. I'm strong enough now to do this on my own."

"No way, baby. You're not getting rid of me that easily." He was stopped from saying anything more by the arrival of the car.

He sniffed unobtrusively and realized someone had put some kind of electronics on it. He could smell nothing explosive or dangerous, just electrical, giving off an intermittent high-frequency whine that was outside the range of human or vamp hearing. But not shifter. Amateurs.

It was probably a tracker. Maybe a listening device, though it seemed to be on the outside of the car, so that was doubtful. Still, he'd be wary. Whatever it was, it had probably been put there on Raintree's orders. Mag would have to stop somewhere and fix that, but for right now, the night was ahead of them and they were in Sin City. Might as well have some fun.

"The night is young. What do you feel like doing? Gambling? Catching a show? Taking a stroll down the strip? Your wish is my command, milady."

"There's a wine bar near the Venetian that stocks Maxwell's wines and some other good vintages. Do you mind if we just go there and take it easy?"

"Do you feel okay?"

"Better than I have in a long time, but as you might imagine, I'm still not quite up to my usual stamina. Still, tonight was a good start."

Mag guided the car through traffic and Miranda gave him more exact directions as they neared their destination. The wine bar was well hidden and obviously catered to an elite clientele. There were a lot of secret places like this all over Vegas that were meant for the really high rollers. Mag knew most of them, but shifters usually left wine bars like this for the vamps.

He parked the car in the public lot on purpose. It was in the open when he used his cell phone to send a few well-placed texts. It was time he called in a few favors from members of his Clan. They wouldn't ask why he needed his car picked up and swept for electronic devices. They'd just do it and report the results. That was the beauty of being part of a shifter Clan. Especially one with as many diverse skills as the Redstone Clan.

Another text summoned their ride home. Something that couldn't be tampered with or traced too easily. Mag smiled as they entered the bar.

The lighting was low, but again, no problem for his enhanced night vision. A pianist tinkled the ivories from a small stage set only a step or two above an empty dance floor. There was a long, gleaming bar along the right hand wall as they entered with groups of people sitting on stools and drinking from shiny crystal glasses. A few steps down to the left led to a more private seating area with booths and tables set around the small dance floor and stage.

Mag had a quiet sniff around and didn't scent any Others. No other shifters. No other vamps. Just humans. Wealthy, highly civilized humans.

Mag kept his arm loosely around Miranda's waist as they were led to a dark corner by a hostess who had greeted Miranda by name. She was known here. Mag filed that information away in his mind. Vamps usually kept a low profile in their hunting grounds, so this probably wasn't a place Miranda came to feed. There had to be some other draw.

A perfectly chilled bottle of wine was delivered to their table a few moments later. All Miranda had to do was nod at the bartender and it was on its way.

"You must come here a lot," Mag observed.

"I do. In fact, I'm one of the owners. Though not a lot of people know that, so keep it under your hat."

"My lips are sealed, sweetheart. But why invest in a human business. I don't sense any Others here. What gives?" He kept his voice so low that only the two of them could hear his frankly worded question.

"It suits me," she answered somewhat flippantly, taking a long sip of her wine.

At that moment, some unseen lighting person was bringing up a subtle spotlight on the little stage in front of the pianist. A young woman took the stage as if she belonged there. She sat on a stool situated in the curve of the piano and a microphone was set up before her. She was elegant and sleek in a long, shimmering black dress, and her features were familiar. Looking from the human girl to Miranda and back again, Mag could see the resemblance, though he knew humans would be susceptible to Miranda's vampire magic and would never see her features all that clearly.

"Who is she?" he asked, almost fearing the answer. He knew Miranda was young for a bloodletter, but he didn't know her exact age.

Miranda smiled softly. "She is my grandniece. My sister's granddaughter."

"She's the reason you invested in this place."

Miranda gave him a wicked grin. "She's the owner. I'm merely the silent partner. My girl has a wicked head for business in addition to her lovely singing voice."

At that moment, the girl on stage began to sing an old torch song. *Skylark* had never sounded so beautiful. Mag sat back to listen, his shifter hearing picking up every nuance of the girl's exceptional voice. If he didn't know better, he'd say she was part siren.

"Magic?" Mag tilted his head, listening carefully. He wasn't as sensitive to magic as some others he knew, but his hearing was keen and there was definitely something different about the woman on stage.

"She has no idea, but I always believed her father was part

nymph or maybe sprite. Something magical, but I'm not sure exactly what. He had the most amazing voice. She's inherited his gift. My side of the family didn't have any magic that I know of. We were completely normal before me." Her tone was wistful and held a trace of regret, if Mag wasn't mistaken.

The song ended and it was clear the singer had noticed them sitting in the dark corner. She stepped off the small stage while the pianist took the spotlight. Her pretty face was wreathed in smiles as she approached their table, holding out both hands to Miranda.

"And how is my favorite fairy godmother? I haven't seen you in ages." The young woman bent down to kiss Miranda on the cheek as they embraced lightly.

Mag stood, politely pulling out a chair to invite the younger woman to join them. She did, shooting him a quizzical smile. They hadn't yet been introduced, but Miranda took care of that in short order.

"Randi, where have you been? I've been trying to get in touch with you for months. Of course, if this guy is the reason you've been in hiding, then I fully understand." She gave Miranda a playful wink as she smiled in Mag's direction. The younger woman was full of life. Vivacious and bubbly. Mag could see the family resemblance though the Miranda he knew had never been quite this cheerful.

"Melissa Zealand, I'd like you to meet Magnus Redstone." Miranda made the formal introductions.

"Call me Mel." The younger woman reached across the table to shake hands with Mag.

"And you should call me Mag. My full name makes me feel like a comic book villain sometimes." She laughed, as he'd expected, the tinkle of sound washing over him. It was infectious. It was magical. Oh, yeah. This girl had magic in her voice.

"So are you two…?" Mel twirled her finger from Mag to Miranda and back again, a teasing question in her gaze.

"None of your business, Mellie." Miranda slapped playfully at that teasing finger, effectively stopping Melissa's overt snooping. "I'm sorry I haven't been around in a while. I had business out of town. I should've told you, but things just got away from me."

Melissa instantly sobered, her brows drawing together in concern. "That isn't like you, Randi. Is everything okay?"

Miranda smiled to soften the mood. "It's all good now. Mag actually helped me straighten some things out and I'm back on track now." Miranda reached over to place her hand familiarly on Mag's forearm. He covered her hand with his, liking the feel of her voluntarily touching him, even in such an innocent manner.

"Redstone…" Melissa seemed to be thinking, then her eyes lit up. "Are you one of the Redstones from the big construction company? There are all kinds of rumors about the handsome Redstone brothers." Her eyes flashed. "Which one are you?"

Mag had to laugh as he leaned back in his chair. "I'm the middle one. I run a few of the crews. You've probably heard how mean and overbearing my older brothers are. And how lost the younger ones are without my guidance." He sipped his wine, enjoying the way Melissa laughed. There was something so pleasant about any sound she made. He knew it was part of her magic and he realized right away why her business looked to be so successful. She drew people to her with that voice. Drew them right to her little bar.

He also liked the genuine affection and concern he saw in her eyes when she looked at Miranda. The younger woman cared about her relative—though she didn't realize they were related. Miranda wasn't allowed close contact with her mortal family. Once they were changed, bloodletters had to let go of their former identity. They could watch from afar, but never reveal their continued existence to their relations. That had to be hard.

As a shifter, family was hugely important to Mag. He was close to his brothers and would do just about anything for them. As he would for the rest of his extended family, and the Redstone Clan. Loyalty and friendships within the Clan were the ties that bound them all together and kept them going. It was hard for a shifter to survive as a loner. The animal spirit that shared their souls didn't like it. Neither did the human half. Shifters needed contact with other shifters.

The women talked about bar business and current events for a few minutes. Mel assured Miranda that she'd forwarded accounting statements to her banker as per their usual arrangements. Miranda just seemed to want to talk to the girl who was a last link to her mortal family. Mag watched the byplay and knew without being told how much that link meant to Miranda. He'd never heard the whole story about how she'd become a vampire, but he got the feeling it was traumatic.

That she had a grandniece meant it had been only a generation or so since she'd been turned. Not long in the annals of vampire kind. He'd known she was young for her kind, but not how young. She had carried herself with such confidence and outright moxie when they'd met. She had seemed well-rooted in her immortal lifestyle.

They left the bar about an hour later, heading out into the night. When Mag steered Miranda away from the parking area and toward one of the nearby giant casinos, she didn't demur, but followed his lead without question.

They got into a special express elevator that took them up to the roof where the helipad was located. Mag had exchanged a few texts with his brother Bob, who was waiting for them in one of the company helicopters. All the brothers knew how to fly. Grif had made sure they all learned after buying the first Redstone Construction chopper years before.

And indeed, when the elevator doors whooshed open on the roof, the small company chopper was parked on the pad, the Redstone Construction logo emblazoned discretely on the side. Bob was in the pilot's seat and he waved when he saw them.

CHAPTER SIX

"What about your car?" was the only question Miranda asked as they walked toward the grounded bird.

"Raintree bugged it. It's better off here for now. Our people will take care of it."

Her eyebrow rose as she turned to look at him. "I didn't even think to look, but I'm not surprised. Raintree doesn't miss a trick. How did you know?"

Mag tapped his ears, then his nose. "Can't beat *were* senses. Plus, after the reception we got, I kind of expected it. I don't mix much with bloodletters. I leave it to Grif to make nice with the Master. They don't know me and I don't know them. Mutual distrust is a big motivator."

Miranda laughed a bit and shook her head as he opened the door to the smallest of the company's choppers. It could seat five—two in front and three in back. Mag would take the front seat because it made sense to have another pilot near the controls should something happen.

He motioned for Miranda to climb in back. He waited until they were both settled and the door closed before making introductions. He wasn't sure what Bob was going to think of Miranda's continued presence. His brothers known when he'd taken her from that nightmare house, but since then he hadn't exactly volunteered the information about where she was.

Bob was motionless, not yet doing the pre-flight check he needed to run through before starting the chopper.

So. Apparently Bob was going to be a little difficult. Fine. Mag could handle his little brother. He secured the latch and turned to face Bob in the confines of the helicopter.

"Thanks for coming." Mag started the conversation on a friendly basis. Where it went from there was up to Bob.

"Haven't seen you in a long time, bro." Bob's tone held a hint of condemnation.

The Redstone brothers had always been close. Even more so since the murder of their mother. Then, after catching the culprits who had killed her, Mag had gone off on his own without giving any details to his siblings. He knew he had some explaining to do.

"Bob, this is Miranda." He decided to be polite. It also bought him a few more seconds to figure out what to say to his brother.

"Ma'am," Bob nodded in Miranda's direction, for once being a man of few words. That was out of character for the usually loquacious Bob. "Glad to see you looking better."

That was something at least. Bob always did have a big heart. He'd seen how badly Miranda had been treated and even though he was probably pissed at Mag right now, he was still *Bob* enough to notice that Miranda was doing well.

"Thanks," Miranda replied quietly. She seemed shy. She had to know his brothers had been there that night they'd rescued her. Maybe subjecting her to one of them so soon after she'd finally been strong enough to venture out of the house was a mistake. "I can't thank you and your family enough for coming to my rescue," she surprised him by adding, thanking Bob outright for his part in the events of that night. "I owe you all a life debt."

Bob's head quirked. He'd been taken by surprise as well, it seemed, and he smiled a suitably humble smile.

"It was just a matter of being in the right place at the right time, ma'am." Bob backpedaled and Mag figured his younger brother didn't know what to do with a friendly vamp. Especially not one that claimed to owe him such an important thing as a life debt. Miranda seemed to want to argue but Mag looked over at her, knowing he couldn't put off the explanation to his brother any longer.

"I'm sorry to drag you out tonight but Raintree bugged my car. I asked Steve to have one of his guys retrieve it and give it the once-over," Mag started his tale. All the brothers knew who the major players in the local vamp community were, so there was no need to explain who Raintree was. It was important to the Clan that the Redstones keep up peaceful relations with the Others in the area, and they had regular briefings on the various communities in the area. "I figured they'd have a harder time tracking us in the air."

"It can still be done," Miranda put in from the back seat. "All it takes is one old one who can shapeshift into something that flies to follow us."

"We've taken that into consideration," Bob told her. "Steve sent along some of the raptors. They're going to shadow our path, and hopefully they'll spot anything else in the sky with us. I also have orders—I think it's only fair to warn you—to take you directly to the company headquarters. Some of the Clan is waiting there to talk to you both."

"Shit," Mag cursed. He'd hoped to put off the family confrontation until Miranda was a little stronger. "Grif?" he asked, pretty sure his eldest brother was at the core of this interception of his plans.

"Yeah, and the rest. Plus Slade and the priestess. They both want to talk to Miranda."

"Oh, no. Slade is the guy I clawed, isn't he?" Miranda cringed.

"Don't worry. Only his pride was hurt," Bob replied with a grin.

"Nevertheless, I owe him an apology." Miranda seemed to steel herself.

"All right then, let's get this over with," Mag gave in to the inevitable. When the Clan united behind something, they usually got what they wanted. It wouldn't be wise to fight this tonight.

The flight to Redstone Construction's headquarters building on the outskirts of town was uneventful. Bob was a competent pilot and he set them down gently, taking care of the big machine while Mag escorted Miranda into the building and the reception committee that was waiting for them.

Sure enough, everyone was gathered in the large conference room just off the lobby. The doors were propped open and it was clear where Mag and Miranda were meant to go. He took her hand as they walked closer.

"If anything makes you uncomfortable, we'll leave, okay? And damn the consequences. Your health comes first." Mag surprised her with the fervency of his words. She knew how important his family was to him and his willingness to anger them on her behalf was touching in the extreme.

"Don't worry. I'll be okay. We knew this was coming at some point. Better to get it over with sooner than later." She tried to smile for him, but she knew it was probably unconvincing. She was not looking forward to the next few minutes, but it had to be done. She owed the shifters a lot—least of all an explanation. And she also owed at least one of them a very large apology.

Mag held her back from the door for one last long moment, searching her gaze. Finally, she took the decision from him. She tugged her hand free from his and turned to enter the room. Mag was right behind her.

She had thought she was prepared for what awaited her, but she wasn't. There was magic here. Strong magic. It acted as a barrier just past the doorway and she wasn't sure what to do. Miranda stopped short.

"What kind of welcome is this?" Mag demanded.

"Just a precaution." A woman stepped forward out of the small crowd to face them. Miranda recognized her.

"You were at the house that night. You're the witch who

undid the magic circles," she breathed. Her memories of that night were hazy, but she remember the woman. And the guy she'd attacked. Slade, his name was. Miranda searched the room but didn't have to look far to see the big man with the eerie blue eyes. He moved to stand behind the woman. Protecting her back.

"As you can see, I can undo the barriers or put them up. In this case, I thought it safer to see what was going on with you and Mag first. After the last time, I hope you'll understand my caution." The woman reached upward to cover Slade's hands, which were now on her shoulders. "I'm Kate, by the way."

"I'm Miranda. And I owe you greatly for freeing me that night. I must also apologize to you, sir." Miranda looked directly at Slade, meeting his spooky gaze without flinching. She refused to show weakness in this room full of predators. That would be a very bad way to start. "My only excuse is that I was not myself when I attacked you. I thought perhaps you both were friends of my captor, come to torment me some more. It wasn't until I heard Mag's voice that I realized your intent wasn't evil. I'm sorry I attacked you and am gratified to see I did no lasting damage. Regardless, I owe you a life debt for freeing me and not killing me when you had the chance."

Miranda bowed her head in acknowledgment of her very serious words. A life debt was not something easily earned or given. She literally owed her rescuers her life. And in the case of these two, she owed them even more than that. She had attacked and nearly killed the man who had freed her. That mistake would haunt her for the rest of her life, and she needed to find a way to make it up to him.

The magic circle that had kept her from fully entering the room shimmered and collapsed. Kate stepped forward and held out her hands to Miranda.

"Be welcome here, Miranda," she said.

Miranda took Kate's hands reflexively and felt the immense magic of the woman. Magic…and goodness. This was a priestess. A real priestess with all the power of her calling and then some. Miranda looked up to meet Kate's gaze and was pinned in place as the priestess's eyes seemed to peer right inside her soul.

"Thank you," Miranda whispered, shaken by the presence of the holy woman and the sheer goodness of her magic.

"I'm sorry to have doubted you, Miranda. Forgive me for remembering only the damage done to my mate. I put up the circle to prevent you from attacking but I see now that attack is the farthest thing from your mind. I would recognize it if you were of evil intent."

"Slade is your mate?" Miranda's heart sank. This just got worse and worse. She'd attacked the priestess's *mate*.

"I am." Slade stepped out from behind Kate and held out one hand in friendship, surprising Miranda.

She took it and felt his odd power. He was intensely magical for a shifter and his blue eyes...glowed...for a brief moment when their gazes met. Miranda felt like a butterfly on a pin, about to go under the microscope. She gulped reflexively, but kept her spine stiff. She had to face these shifters on their own ground and not show the fear that made her knees tremble. A true vampire wouldn't be afraid of these people, but she owed them and they were Mag's family. His Clan. She wouldn't do anything to hurt them in any way, including insulting them. In fact, some part of her wanted to make a good impression on them, but she didn't examine what drove that impulse too closely.

"I am so sorry about attacking you," she repeated, holding his hand and hoping he could see how earnest her apology was. "I feel awful about it."

"I will admit, you took me by surprise and bruised my ego, but it all worked out and everything's okay. I understand why you did it, even if I didn't appreciate it at the time. In fact, you showed a great deal of restraint to be able to pull back from the killing impulse that runs so strong in your race."

His words were gracious and gave her way too much credit. She drew her hand away and turned to glance at Mag, who stood at her side.

"Don't give me the credit on that. It's all due to Mag. His voice is what got through to me. Otherwise, I'm really afraid of what would have happened. I probably would've continued trying to kill you, and your people would have ripped me apart." She looked around the room, including them all in her words. "I don't blame any of you. I was crazed at the time. There's not much else you can do with an insane bloodletter except kill them and put them out of their misery—and to keep the rest of the world safe. I'm glad you were prepared to do that for me and I'm equally glad Mag was there to bring me back from the brink."

"How did he manage that, exactly?" A tall, fair-haired shifter stepped forward to stand beside Slade. She recognized him instantly. This was the eldest. The Alpha.

"I knew Mag from before I was captured. About two years ago, we met and spent exactly one evening together. I drank from him. Which I think you know forms a small bond—especially when the person I drink from has magic of their own. Mag and I will have that bond 'til the day one of us leaves this realm. He was…very special to me."

"You don't have to tell them any of this, sweetheart." Mag touched her arm, defending her even against his closest family. She couldn't come between them. She loved him too much to allow her presence to harm his relationship with his family, if she could help it. "This is none of their business."

"It is our business, Mag. Nobody has seen you for weeks, and suddenly you're mixed up with dangerous vamps tracking your movements?" Grif was clearly agitated as he ran one hand through his short hair, and his voice rose.

"Is this some kind of intervention?" Mag looked around the room and chuckled, clearly seeing the humor in this gathering, even if nobody else did. Miranda smiled with him and knew they had to clear the air with his family as soon as possible. They were truly worried about him.

"They love you," she cautioned, putting one hand on his chest as she turned to him. "They deserve answers."

"You don't deserve to be treated like a criminal," he replied, his gaze holding hers. But she smiled.

"No, Mag. They're just concerned. They have a right to be. Our…friendship…is forbidden by both our peoples. We both knew that going in."

"Are you sleeping with her?" Grif demanded. His anger clearly hadn't abated. If anything, it had escalated.

"That's really none of your damn business," Mag answered back, stepping around Miranda to confront his oldest brother. The rest of the shifters in the room bristled— except for Slade, who watched the byplay with keen interest.

"Gentlemen." Miranda stepped between them, one palm out to ward off each of the big men. Not that she could really do anything if they decided to mix it up. Sure, she was a vampire, but she was still weak as a kitten after her ordeal. Of course, only Mag really knew the extent of her weakness. She appealed to both of them. "I refuse to come between you in any way. If I'm the problem, I'll just remove myself from the equation."

"Like hell you will!" Mag's anger shifted to her, as she'd expected. Good.

"I will and you know it. I did it before and I'll do it again," she promised him in a quiet voice before turning back to Grif and dropping her hands. "To answer your question, we are not having sex, and I don't intend to do so. It's forbidden, as you well know. I left him two years ago, and I'd do it again if necessary."

"Yet simply hearing his voice pulled you out of a killing rage?" Kate asked, her gaze shrewd. "I think there's more between you than a simple fling."

"Maybe there is," Miranda squared her shoulders and faced the priestess, unable to lie to her outright. "But as I said, it's forbidden. I'm too young a bloodletter to break that rule. I'd be dead before morning if any of my brethren found out I had a steady supply of shifter blood, and you all know it."

"Now we come to the crux of it." Kate smiled though

Miranda couldn't imagine what there was to smile about in this situation. "It's not that you're forbidden by some arcane rule of magic, it's that your fellow bloodletters don't want anyone upsetting the hierarchy by having access to magical blood. Isn't that right?"

"Well, don't shifters have a similar rule? I was under the impression your kind didn't allow your people to mix with bloodletters on a regular basis." Miranda didn't know where the priestess was going with this, but she'd follow along for now.

"Like your people, we have a set hierarchy based on relative strength, for the most part," Grif spoke, rejoining the conversation. "In our Clan, we have a somewhat extended power structure because any one of my brothers could rule the entire Clan. We're all Alphas. Under normal circumstances, we probably would have gone off in different directions to form our own familial Clans. But the Redstone Clan is bigger than just cougars. We have all sorts of shifters under our umbrella and in our employ. The company *is* the Clan, in many respects, and vice versa," Grif clarified, calming as the priestess guided the conversation.

"There's no outright prohibition against shifters having vampire mates," Slade added. "But there are consequences. The shifter gains from the exchange of fluids too. They heal faster. They gain strength and speed. Things like that. While the vampire in the couple gains the power of her shifter mate."

"How do you know this?" Miranda was shocked. Here they were, talking about mixed mating as if it was fact, and not just forbidden fantasy.

"There have been mixed matings in the past, you know," Slade winked at her.

"Actually, I don't know anything of the kind. Where did you learn this?" She really was intrigued now. Intrigued, and feeling rather as if she'd been blindsided. Were they saying there was a way for her and Mag to be together? She almost didn't dare hope.

"It's in our histories. Far back, when the forces of Light stood against the darkness. When Elspeth roamed this realm with her supporters who later became the *Venifucus*. When she tried to rule the world, and was damned to the farthest realms for the destruction and devastation she caused." Kate recited the words as if they came out of a history book. Maybe they had. The priestesses had access, it was said, to a vast store of knowledge not entrusted to any Others. "When Elspeth last threatened us all, much power was given by the Goddess to a few, very special people who served Her in the fight against the darkness. So it's not completely unheard of for a shifter and a bloodletter to mate. It has been done in the past."

"In the distant past," Miranda countered, unable to really believe where this conversation was going.

"And in the present," Slade added quietly. "Have you ever heard of a very old bloodletter called Dante d'Angleterre?"

"I've heard of him, but I don't know him," Miranda confirmed. Dante was one of the most powerful and reclusive bloodletters in the States.

"He recently found his One. She's a werewolf." Slade gave the news in grave tones.

Miranda didn't know what to say as silence fell in the room. Grif looked surprised. Miranda didn't have the courage to turn and see what Mag might be thinking.

"When were you two going to tell me this?" Grif demanded, but not in an angry way. He seemed more amused than annoyed.

"We just got confirmation," Kate said. "I talked to the High Priestess before we left the house."

Miranda started to panic. "Why are we talking about mating?" she asked in a shaky voice. "Nobody said anything about mating." She backed up a step but Mag was there, his arm going around her shoulders, halting her retreat and offering comfort.

"It's okay, sweetheart. Everybody," he addressed his family and friends. "Thank you for your concern, but I really think you're going too far here and presuming too much. Miranda has had a hell of a time since she was freed. Tonight was her first night out and so far, it's been a doozy. I asked for help with my car, not with anything else, and much as I appreciate your concern, I think we'll be going now."

"Not so fast," Grif spoke just as Mag turned with his arm still around Miranda. Bob was standing in the doorway and he didn't look likely to move without some kind of altercation. Miranda heard Mag sigh as he turned back to his eldest brother.

"What now? Feel like interrogating a woman who's still recovering from months of captivity and torture just for fun? I warn you, if you keep on with this, I'll fight you."

The rest of the room went deathly quiet. Open defiance of one's brother was one thing, but open defiance of the Clan Alpha was quite another.

Luckily, it appeared Grif wasn't a hothead. He seemed to think through his words before speaking.

"Miranda, I apologize if this all seems heavy handed. We don't mean to put you through any more difficulties. To the contrary, you have friends among my Clan—and one very big protector in my brother. That's clear. What I wanted to accomplish by cornering you both, was to find out what's going on, and what we can do to help. I'll admit, I also wanted to get a better read on you. It's not often that my brother spends so much time away from the family, holed up with a woman. And our introduction to you was violent, to say the least." Grif tempered his words with a half-grin that she found endearing. She could easily see the resemblance between the brothers. "Please sit down. We won't keep you long, but I think a few points need to be clarified."

Miranda could see that Grif wasn't going to budge and now that he was being polite, she didn't see a way to refuse. She didn't want to come between Mag and his family. She'd have to see this thing through to the end. Moving forward without waiting for Mag to follow, she took a seat at the wide conference table.

CHAPTER SEVEN

"Let's get on with this, shall we?" She saw their surprise when she took the bull by the horns. "We've already established that I'm not sleeping with Mag. He's been taking care of me. Nursing me back to health, in fact. I took his blood only on the night of the rescue. Since then, I've had a steady diet of blood-laced wine on the advice of someone named Sebastian, who I believe is a friend of yours." She looked rather pointedly down the table to the youngest looking of the five sandy-haired men in the room. All five of the Redstone brothers were gathered together and she took it as a sort of weird compliment that the other four had come to see about the vampire in Mag's life. "You're Matt, right? Thanks for hooking Mag up with your friend. His advice has worked wonders." She was a big proponent of giving credit where it was due.

Matt nodded to her, then met Grif's questioning gaze.

"Is this true, Matt?" Grif asked, betraying the fact that not all the brothers had been communicating every point where she was concerned. Interesting.

"Sebastian is a friend," was Matt's reply. "Mag asked for help and I got it for him."

Grif nodded with a tight movement. "As it should be. I just wasn't aware you were still in such close contact with your bloodletter pals in Napa."

"They're *friends*, Grif. We stay in touch. And if I need help, they're there." Matt paused for a moment before adding. "Just like I'm there for them."

Wow. So Mag hadn't been kidding when he said his little brother had close ties with a few, select bloodletters. Sounded like he was a loyal friend to Sebastian and perhaps some of the others in the hierarchy of the Napa Valley vamps. She wondered what they had done to earn such loyalty and vice versa, but that was a question for another time.

"What happened tonight?" Grif changed the subject. "This was your first night out since the rescue, right?"

Miranda nodded. "I knew my first duty was to report to the leadership. I'm too young to flout their rules. Mag took me into town, and I chose to go to Raintree's."

"The vamp bar?" Grif asked, as well informed as she'd expected. "How'd that go?"

"Raintree wasn't pleased by the company I'm keeping, but he's only the second in command. I expect a summons from the Master any time now. It'll be up to him if any action is to be taken." She knew her duty, and though she hated to think of the consequences of that summons, she also knew she couldn't go against the Master with impunity. If he said to leave Mag, she'd have to leave him, no matter how much it broke her heart. Again.

Mag had taken a seat at her side. Mercifully, he took over the explanation. "Everything was going okay until we left. Miranda had her first real meal in months, and I managed not to kill the guy," Mag chuckled, but it was a dark sound. She heard the truth in his admission, though he'd meant to mask it with a joke. She'd known he hadn't liked watching her feed from another man, but he had to know the human prey she'd fed from meant nothing to her. She would make that clear to him, once they were alone.

"Raintree—or someone at the club, probably working on his orders—definitely bugged your car." Another of the brothers spoke after glancing at his smart phone. He was probably the second eldest, Steve. He was the one Mag had said was in charge of security and had men that were going to pick up the car and check it over. "Both GPS and audio. They were very thorough," Steve reported. "My guys took your car to a jobsite in the city. It'll stay there until we're sure we got everything."

Mag nodded at Steve. "Thanks, bro. I owe you one."

"So I take this to mean that your people don't really know where you've been staying?" Grif took over the questioning again.

"They haven't known where I've been since before I was taken prisoner," Miranda replied, a bit of her bitterness coming through in her tone, though she fought for neutrality. "I'm not very important in the hierarchy. I'm too young to really be on anyone's radar. They don't consider me a threat. More likely, they expect me to do something stupid and end up truly dead sooner rather than later. Most of the young ones do, or so I've been told." She tried to be nonchalant about it, but she had a real fear of dying so ingloriously, with no one to mourn or even mark her passing.

"Why all the interest now? Is it because of Mag?" Grif asked astutely.

"Undoubtedly," she agreed. "To them, I'm young and probably stupid, but suddenly I'm keeping company with a shifter. Now I need to be watched." She couldn't hide her bitterness that time. "Nobody gave a damn when I disappeared. They probably thought I was gone for good, and not one of them cared to find out for sure. Nobody was looking for me. I either turned up again—or not. They didn't care either way. But when I turned up with Mag, they damn well took notice. Now I'm interesting. And maybe a threat." She was getting pissed off just thinking about it. Her people were cold. Not physically, maybe, but inside, they were cold as ice.

"Are you a threat?" Grif asked in a very careful voice that calmed her right down.

She took a deep breath. "No," she answered in a quiet,

strong voice. "I'm not a threat to anyone. Not to them. Not to you. The only person I have issues with is the evil mage who captured me—and those like him. After what I've suffered, and when I regain my strength fully, if I run across evil, I'm going to do my damndest to stop it."

"I knew it." Kate smiled as she seemed to light up from within. "I see the goodness in you, you know. It's why I dropped the shield. It's why I forgave you for hurting my mate. The Lady's Light shines in your soul now, Miranda, and She guides your steps. You have been tested by Her fire and have come out stronger."

"If those months of torture and starvation were some kind of test, please tell your Lady I didn't really appreciate it," Miranda answered with a bit of reluctant humor.

She was pleased by the priestess's praise, but wasn't sure what to make of her words. Miranda didn't feel any different inside. She'd always tried to be a good person—before and after her change to drinking blood to survive. She'd never killed anyone who didn't deserve it, and she didn't think she ever would.

Becoming a vampire had given her killer instincts, but they'd always been tempered by her human heart. The others thought her weak because of it, but she had always thought her compassion made her strong. The killers among her kind were the weak ones. They couldn't stand against the instincts that drove them. They gave in and deluded themselves into believing that was ultimate power. To her way of thinking, that was ultimate evil—to give in to the darkness, to take the easy route.

Grif sighed and took control of the conversation once more. "The priestess speaks well for you, and Slade seems to concur. I respect their opinions." Grif nodded at the mated pair who both seemed to give their approval of Miranda, much to her shock. "You also seem to be recovering well in Mag's care, and he apparently found out what to do for you from Matt's friend. I see no real reason you can't go on as you were, regaining your strength." He turned his gaze to

Mag. "I know you haven't been on Clan lands and I think that's wise for now. Many of our people aren't fond of bloodletters. But you have my approval and backup when you need it, Mag. As usual. I just needed to see for myself what was going on and meet your lady, now that she's able to speak for herself."

"Fair enough," Mag acknowledged his brother's ruling. "I'm sorry I didn't come to you before, but I wasn't sure of our welcome."

"And you wanted to keep her to yourself a bit longer." Grif smiled. "That's okay. I understand. But you really need to trust me a little more. We are family, after all." He stood and came around the table as everyone else got to their feet. He shook Mag's hand and pulled him in for a big hug. Shifters were very tactile—something her own people were not.

He let his brother go and turned to her, offering her a hand in friendship. She was surprised—and pleased. The Alpha of one of the most powerful shifter Clans in the country was way above her pay grade, but he didn't seem to look down on her at all. In fact, if anything, he seemed openly accepting of her and friendly. She was floored. And honored.

She took his hand and met his gaze. "Thank you for your welcome and I meant what I said. I owe you and your Clan a life debt I will never forget. You saved me when you could have as easily ended me, and been well within your rights to do so. I cannot thank you enough, Alpha."

"One thing you need to understand about my family and my Clan. We serve the Light. We take our vows to the Mother of All very seriously and we don't kill unless we must. I'm glad we were in the right place at the right time, and that Mag was able to pull you back from the edge. He's the one you should thank. You have the protection of my Clan for as long as you need to heal, Miranda."

She was doubly impressed. The Alpha had just given her something few outsiders were ever granted. Protection of the Clan was not something to shrug off. She shook his hand with deep respect.

"You are a kind man, Griffon Redstone. Thank you for your understanding." She reached up and kissed him on the cheek, unable to contain her emotional response. She knew she surprised him, but he didn't back away, and that little sign of trust meant the world to her. A tear was in her eye when she stepped back, releasing his hand.

The meeting broke up and people were talking among themselves a bit, now that the potential crisis had been averted. Kate and Slade came up to her and Mag stepped to one side to consult with his brother Steve—probably over arrangements for his car. Kate snagged her attention as Grif moved away.

"It's not forbidden if you want to renew your relationship with Mag. It might help you heal faster, in fact," Kate said without preamble, diving right in where angels feared to tread.

"It's almost like cheating," Miranda answered without revealing her real reasons. "And shifter blood can be addictive, from what I hear. I'd rather not become dependent. This thing with Mag can only be temporary. Shifters might— and I emphasize *might*—accept me, but I doubt the Master would welcome a jumped up youngster in his domain."

"Tony might surprise you," Slade put in, using the Master's nickname. She was a little taken aback. Did this oddly magical shifter know the Master well enough to be on a first-name basis? He just might. And she'd clawed him. Darnit. She still felt awful about it, and could barely meet his penetrating blue gaze.

"Just know that it's not forbidden. It never was. The Lady would not let you find your mate only to deny him to you. She doesn't do that to Her servants. And you, my new friend, will most definitely be one of the Lady's servants in time. I'm not all that clairvoyant, but I can see the glow of your spirit and it's very familiar to me. Give it some thought."

Miranda's eyes widened and her first instinct was denial. She wasn't worthy of such thoughts. She was a vampire. A killer. One who had to fight her instincts every time she fed. She was no angel. She was a predator. One of the deadliest that walked the earth. Even weak as she was right now, she was still dangerous, and she could never forget it. She could never lose control again. She'd almost killed Slade the last time she'd lost it, and she'd have to live with that for the rest of her life.

Mag came back and put his hand on her shoulder, joining their small group. He hadn't heard what Kate had said, but he definitely clued in to Miranda's mood. His hand rubbed little, comforting circles on her shoulder, squeezing gently.

Kate turned her attention to Mag. "I think she should feed from you," the priestess said bluntly. "She needs to regain her strength—and then some—before you face that summons from the Master. They need to see what she can become. They can't see her weak. Do you understand?" She seemed very insistent on that point. Miranda was confused. So, it appeared, was Mag when Miranda turned to gauge his expression.

"I'll take good care of her, Kate. Thanks for your concern." He wouldn't say any more on the subject and for that, Miranda was glad. Kate had sewn a seed of temptation in her mind and she found herself contemplating drinking from Mag as they took their leave. Bob met them at the door and led them to a big SUV waiting in the drive.

The men talked security measures for a moment while Miranda took her seat on the passenger side of the dark vehicle. She heard something about raptors following their path and being stationed around the house, but she mostly tuned out their conversation as thoughts of drinking from Mag filled her mind. It was such a temptation. Such a lure.

Why would the priestess and her mate tell her such things about d'Angleterre and his new werewolf mate, and those other unions in the distant past? Was it really true?

Miranda knew the *Venifucus* were back. She'd heard enough about them from her captor. She knew he'd worked for them, and that he had friends among their evil number.

She had sworn vengeance on the ancient group if she was ever freed, and she would follow that path as soon as she regained her strength. But if the *Venifucus* were back, and working toward restoring Elspeth to this realm, were the ancient unions between shifter and bloodletter going to make a comeback too?

They'd told her those ancient powerful unions had been allied against the *Venifucus* in the last battle against Elspeth. Miranda was already against them and she thought Mag was too. They'd discussed how the mage who had held her prisoner had been part of the team that had murdered his mother. From all reports, the Clan had caught and brought to justice both of the mages who had killed the Redstone matriarch, but the *Venifucus* were an ongoing threat. Others had been targeted by their agents, and each day new reports seemed to come in about their plots.

Mag had kept her informed while she recovered, telling her about different events in the wider world of shifters. He'd told her about the attack on the new High Priestess and a few other incidents that had happened in other shifter Packs and Clans. It was something to talk about while she recovered. Something that wasn't as explosive as other topics— especially the topic of their relationship.

Mag drove home while her mind raced a mile a minute. He didn't say much until they were well away from the Redstone Construction building and on the road toward his place in the desert.

"I'm sorry about that." He spoke quietly, not upsetting the delicate balance of the desert night. "My family, I mean. I didn't think they'd ambush us until later."

"It's okay. We both knew it was coming," she allowed. "And it's clear they were worried about you. I don't blame them for wanting to meet the wicked woman monopolizing all your nights." She giggled a little at the thought of that. If only it was as naughty as it sounded.

She'd spent one night in his arms two years ago, and it had ruined her for any other man. She hadn't had sex with anyone since him. Even though she brought many of her prey males to completion through sheer vampire magic alone—because it made their blood so much more powerful if she drank at their moment of climax—she hadn't been tempted to join any of them in the moment.

She still wanted Mag. She always wanted him. He was her One, though she'd firmly shut the connection that had tried to open between them during that one moment of shared ecstasy. Even as young as she was, she had more skill with psychic magic than Mag did. Shifters weren't very psychic generally, but vamps had all sorts of skills in that area.

Miranda had worked hard on her abilities when she'd first been turned. She had perfected one of the basic skills all baby vamps were taught—keeping your mind to yourself. She was able to shut down and keep people out. Maybe not an ancient bloodletter who was way more powerful than she was, but certainly a mortal or a shifter who had no real psychic abilities.

That would change though, if she allowed the mating. If she eased the iron control she kept over the place in her mind where they were connected, she and Magnus would share their minds. They'd be able to communicate silently, and share their thoughts and memories.

If she dared.

Miranda didn't know if she had the nerve for it. It was a frightening thought. Something many vampires waited centuries to find. It seemed unreal that she'd found her One after only a little more than half a century as a bloodletter, and without even really bothering to look.

Could the priestess be right? Could the Mother of All have had a hand in their meeting? Was there some big plan in place to get them together?

Miranda was afraid. If there was an element of fate in their finding each other, what sort of destiny could that mean for them, if those ancient couples were fighters in the war against Elspeth? Was war coming once again? And if so, would they be on the front lines of it?

Miranda hadn't been born a fighter, but she knew herself well enough now to know she'd be ready if it came. Kate had been right in implying that the ordeal she'd suffered had changed her. It had tested her and tempered her. She knew who her enemies were, and why she had to fight them. She could not let others suffer as she had at the hands of their madness and evil.

"Speaking of nights," Mag recaptured her wandering attention. "I'm pretty sure we'll be facing the Master tomorrow night. In fact, I'm surprised we didn't get the summons right after we left Raintree's."

"Bloodletters move fast when they want to, but immortality can sometimes give them—especially the really old ones—a sort of lethargy. They move at their own pace and do things when it suits them. After all, there's always tomorrow night, right? I think when you live that long, time starts to become almost meaningless." It was her own little theory, but she'd seen a lot in the past fifty or sixty years to prove it was true.

"I know it's rude to ask a lady her age, but I keep hearing how young you are for a vamp. So what have you got— almost a century? Less?"

She had to laugh. "Not quite that much. I was born mortal in 1932 and changed in my twenties. If I had not been changed, I'd be in my eighties now. Instead, I'm perpetually twenty-two years old. Frozen in time." She sighed and looked out the window at the passing desert scenery. It was stark in the night, but still beautiful in an austere way. "My little sister, Ainsley, is still alive. She's in her late seventies and still going strong. She looks so much like our mother did. I wish I could talk to her, but I've done my best to watch over her and her family through the years. She named her daughter after me and then little Miranda got married and had Melissa."

The car pulled in to a long driveway. They were already back at Mag's place. Time had flown while she contemplated so many difficult things—her family, Mag's family, the words of the priestess and her mate... Miranda was terribly confused by it all.

Mag got out and came around to open her door, ushering her up the walk. A shimmer in front of them solidified into a naked man and Mag didn't even blink. Instead, he tossed the guy the keys and continued on his way.

"Who was that? And where did he come from?" Miranda looked over her shoulder as the guy opened the back door of the SUV. He retrieved some clothing that had been stashed back there and got dressed. A few moments later, she heard the engine start and the vehicle roll away, back down the drive.

"One of Steve's guys. A raptor. He flew here, following us. That little nod he gave me? That was the signal that the coast was clear. We weren't followed. Nor has anyone strange been prowling around the house. He no doubt already checked in with the guys Steve put on the roof, and Billy over there." Mag pointed toward the side of the house where a big dog stood silhouetted against the sky for a short moment. Only it wasn't a dog. It was a wolf. A werewolf. Had to be.

Between one moment and the next, the wolf had disappeared back into the night. He'd come out of hiding just long enough to make his presence known, then faded away again, a true master of stealth. Miranda could feel the slight tingle of shifter magic, but other than that, she wouldn't have been aware of his presence at all.

An owl hooted and she looked up to find a massive creature staring at her from the peak of the roof. Mag waved at it with a friendly gesture. The owl was another shifter, showing his or her presence before stepping back into the shadows.

"As you can see, we'll be well guarded. The Clan won't let any bloodletters—or anything else for that matter—mess with us. That's just one of the perks of being part of a Clan."

"They'd do this for any Clan member? I mean, it's not just because you're part of the ruling family, right?" Miranda was impressed.

"Oh, most definitely." He ushered her through the door

and rearmed the security system. "We do the same for all Clan members who need a little extra help. We're a big family and the hierarchy only matters in deciding who gives the orders. I'm an Alpha, so in any gathering of lesser shifters, I run the show. Same for my brothers, and the other Alphas we have in the Clan. There's a hierarchy among the wolves, for example, and a single Alpha who rules over all of them. And the owls, and the hawks, and so on. All of those leaders come under Grif's rule, though. They form a sort of advisory council that meets once a month or whenever there's need. If the wolves have a problem they can't solve among themselves, their Alpha goes to Grif and he either solves it or delegates it to one of us who has particular expertise in whatever the problem is. Like how Steve handles all the security stuff. He's the acknowledged expert on that kind of thing, though we all have some training and interest."

"It's a lot more complicated than I thought. Are all shifter groups like that?" They walked together through the living room while Mag seemed to be inspecting every window and door as they passed.

"The Redstone organization is unique in the States. We're the biggest and we have the largest variety of species under our banner. Grif built both the Clan and the business into something I don't think any of us really expected, but it works. Grif is a great leader. Other Alphas—myself included—are happy to follow him. He's fair, and has a really brilliant mind for strategy, which means prosperity in business and safety for Clan members. And after all, isn't that really the American dream? Prosperity, safety and the freedom to be what you are in your own domain. Just another way of saying *life, liberty, and the pursuit of happiness*. That's what Redstone Construction and the Redstone Clan means to its members."

"You're quite the public relations man," Miranda observed and he started to chuckle. She shot him a questioning look.

"PR is one of my responsibilities for the company," he admitted. "Each of us runs a department or two in addition to working some of the jobs or crews. Steve got Security. Grif is the CEO. Bob runs Finance. Matt does what would otherwise be called Human Resources. We just call it Personnel. And I do the schmoozing. I make it rain, bringing in some of the really big deals and handle what little advertising and public relations we need."

"So you're the Sales department? How'd you end up with that?" She smiled, surprised by his role in the company. He seemed so brawny and tough. She couldn't imagine him wining and dining some fat cat developer in order to get a job contract for the company.

"Well, we all participate when we want to go after a really big contract, but I make all the arrangements. I do the pitches and work up the drawings and models. I keep track of all the scheduling and project management. You see, I'm an architect." He admitted it like it was some sort of big secret. And really, it was. She hadn't had any idea of his educational background.

"No wonder your house is so gorgeous." It was the first thought that popped into her mind and apparently it was the right thing to say. He smiled as he led her into another room, which looked like his office. She hadn't been in there before. There was the usual desk and files, but there was also a big drafting table with sketches on it. She went right over to it and marveled at the structure she saw drawn in bold strokes on the white paper. "You designed this?"

He nodded as he joined her at the table. "It's an idea I've had for a while. The whole structure is meant to run on solar and geothermal power. Very green. Some of our clients in California are interested in these kinds of designs."

"I bet. This is gorgeous as well as practical." She turned to him, smiling. "As is this house. You designed it as well, didn't you?"

"It's not perfect," he was quick to say as he looked around the room. "I designed it to be a sunny oasis in the desert and had to retrofit it for the sun-proofing, but it worked out. It would have been better to design a sun-proof house from the ground up, but I'm pleased with the results here and now I know the best methods to incorporate into future designs. Do you think any of your bloodletter friends would be in the market for a new lair?" he asked comically, pulling her away from the drafting table and into his arms. "It could be a whole new line of business for the company. What do you think?"

"It could work." She tilted her head, grinning at him. "If they could be persuaded to trust you. Sadly, bloodletters aren't very trusting people, in general."

"Except you, sweetheart. You trust me, don't you?" He tugged her closer and leaned his head downward so that his lips were only an inch from hers. Her body craved the contact, loving the feel of his strong, hard-muscled form against her.

"I'm young and foolish, remember?" she teased, closing the gap between them, sealing their lips in a kiss she'd wanted for so very long.

CHAPTER EIGHT

She couldn't pull back. She couldn't put an end to this sublime feeling. Being in Mag's arms was like nothing else. It was everything. It was pure pleasure and all that was right with the world. How could she continue to deny herself when he was right there, clearly wanting to kiss her as much as she wanted him to.

She arched up into his kiss, giving more, taking more, demanding all and giving it back in return. Her body strained against his, wanting to be closer, annoyed by the layers of clothing that separated them.

She gasped when he broke their lips apart and swung her up into his arms. He carried her out of the office and down the hall to the room where she'd spent the majority of her time asleep since being freed. But she wasn't asleep now. No, she was as far from sleep as it was possible to get. Her body revved up with the wonder of its mate's caresses.

He lay her on the bed like an offering to some pagan deity and she went willingly. When his hard body came down over hers, she welcomed him, straining upward to meet his renewed kiss. Their breathing increased as their bodies moved in rhythm, pleasure blossoming between them. She couldn't let this go much further if she wanted to retain control over their psychic link. If she came, she wouldn't be able to keep the connection closed off, and he'd know. They'd be linked again, and she would find it close to impossible to close that connection.

She pushed against his chest, knowing what had to be and hating it with all her heart.

"Mag, we can't do this," she panted as he moved back a few inches, allowing her to speak.

"I'm not leaving you tonight, Miranda. I can't. Please don't ask me to." His grip tightened and then he suddenly rolled away, sitting up on the side of the bed, his hands running through his hair.

She understood. She felt the same. It was hell denying their connection, but she didn't see any alternative in which they both survived the experience of giving in to it.

"Watching you feed from that guy in the club tonight…" His voice held a world of pain and jealousy. "It was the last straw for me. I can't watch that again. I won't be able to keep myself from tearing your prey apart. Do you understand? You're my *mate*, Miranda. I don't know what that means among bloodletters, but among shifters, mates are sacred. Blessed. Protected and cherished. Mates are forever, Miranda." His voice dropped to a whisper as he turned to her as their gazes met. "I want forever with you."

Oh, dear Goddess. Her heart broke at the look in his eyes, and her heart echoed with the pain she also felt. How could she hurt him this way? How could she hurt them both with her continued denial of their bond?

Knowing he felt it too broke down all her barriers. She'd thought she was the only one who knew about their connection, but she should've known better. Shifters had magic all their own, and even if they didn't know their One the same way her people did, they probably had some way of identifying their life mate. She'd been so stupid.

"I'm sorry." Her voice cracked as emotion swamped her. "I thought I could keep the connection closed and you wouldn't be hurt by it. I thought I was the only one suffering. Oh, Mag." She nearly leapt into his arms and clung to him as tears threatened. "I knew you were my One that first night. Our minds touched and I pulled back, hoping you didn't notice." Her confession came out in a rush. "I can't do it anymore, but I don't see how this is going to work. Your people don't like me. My people will probably try to destroy us both rather than let me move up in the hierarchy. I thought staying away from you would protect us both, but all it's done is hurt us. I'm so sorry. Can you forgive me?"

His big hands cupped her head as he drew away to look deep into her eyes. "My love, I know you were doing what you thought was right. So was I, even as I let you go. I could've searched harder for you. Instead, I waited until you came to me and it was almost too late. Can you forgive me for not coming for you sooner?" His voice dropped as pain filled his gaze. "If I had pushed to find you, you would never have been captured. Your ordeal was my fault. I'm the one who needs your forgiveness."

"Oh, Mag, don't ever say that!" She was shocked that he'd take on that kind of guilt over something she had come to see as inevitable. "My ordeal, as you put it, is laid squarely at the feet of the mage who did it. It was never about you, and second guessing our decisions now gets us nowhere. Even if you had found me back then, who's to say I would've gone with you? I would've fought you, just as I've fought this attraction. As my mother used to say, everything happens for a reason. I have to believe that."

"Funny. My mother used to say the same thing." He leaned his forehead against hers as their emotions began to settle. "You know, you're wrong about the Clan. If you're my mate, you're automatically a member of the Clan. That means they will protect you. Just like they protect me—and vice versa. I think they'll come to love you. I mean, what shifter Clan has a pet vampire at their disposal? Think of the entrée that will give us…if you're willing to work with us."

"So it's love me, love my Clan?" She couldn't believe what he was saying. Would it really be possible to live among shifters and not be a detested outsider?

"Something like that." He smiled and drew back, though his arms remained around her, keeping her in the circle of his warmth. "Like I said, a mate is a sacred thing. Most shifters find their mates among their own kind, but there are always outliers. Humans. Mages. Humans with mage ancestors or shifter ancestors. You haven't met her yet, but Grif's mate is like that. She wasn't a shifter until recently—which is a long story for another time—but you should know that she's quickly taking her place as the matriarch of the Clan and everyone loves her. Shifters believe that the Goddess guides us in finding out true mates. Who are we to argue with the Wisdom of the Goddess? If you're my mate—and you are— then nobody can question it. To question our mating would be to question the Mother of All and nobody wants to dare that."

"You think they'd really accept me among them?" A tiny flicker of hope started to form inside her.

"It might take a little time, and they'll be standoffish at first, but they'll accept you. Eventually, they'll protect you like one of their own. It's already starting. Because you *will be* one of them. You'll be Clan. Because you're my mate. It's just that simple for us shifters."

"It's way more complicated among bloodletters," she whispered, knowing there was still a lot of hurdles to overcome, but Mag had given her a sliver of hope, and it continued to grow.

"Then we stay with the Clan. Vamps can't touch you on our lands. And if I understand bloodletter mating correctly, you'll only ever have to drink from me if we mate, right? My blood, and lots and lots of sex will keep you in good health. It'll be tough, but I'll do my part. Especially the sex part." He teased her, and her heart lightened. She was smiling as his lips drew closer.

"You make it sound so simple."

"It is simple. Simple as you and me. We're the only two that matter in the end. Your people. My Clan. That's all just details. The big thing is right here, between us. Our two souls and no one else. What do you say? Will you agree to stay with me and be my mate? Goddess knows I've wanted to be your One since the moment I met you."

She couldn't fight it anymore.

"You are. You've always been my One, Mag." She reached up and twined her arms around his neck, drawing him closer.

Their kiss was one of coming home. Of freedom to be who they really were, and joy at being honest with themselves and each other for the first time.

She thought about letting go of her stranglehold on their psychic connection, but decided to wait. For one thing, it might startle Mag right out of the mood, and she didn't want to wait one more second. For another, she'd lose control soon enough. There was no way she could keep the connection closed through a climax.

Miranda wanted this to be like the first time they made love. Letting the connection happen naturally, at the moment of crisis, would be better. It would be a more natural discovery of her One, without the fear that had swamped her the first time. A new memory for her to start their new life together with—for however long it lasted.

She wasn't as optimistic as he was about how their relationship would work, but she could no longer deny the fact that he was her One. The only One she would ever know. Many bloodletters went centuries before they found theirs, and many never did. She couldn't let him go. Not now. Not when there might be the slightest chance that somehow this impossible relationship might work out.

Not when she loved him with all her heart.

Miranda tugged at his clothing as her heart rate increased. She wanted him now. She didn't want to wait any longer. Foreplay was unnecessary. She'd been in an almost constant state of arousal since the moment she'd tasted his blood back when she was so badly injured she was almost mindless. It had taken all her willpower to stay away from him all this time, but no more. She wanted him and she wanted him now.

Mag moved back, separating them for the short moment it

took to rip his shirt off over his head. Then he was back, kissing her as he worked on her clothing. Separating again to drag her shirt off too, she lifted her arms eagerly to help. The sooner they were naked, the better.

Fabric tore as she pushed at his pants and she had to stifle a laugh. He didn't seem to notice though. His touch was gentler but just as insistent on her. With a few sharp tugs and more ripping sounds, they were both free of the fabric that had kept them apart.

Mag leaned over her as he lowered her to the bed. His perfect body covered hers and she gladly made room for him between her legs, welcoming him with every gesture, every mewling sound of need she couldn't suppress. He didn't disappoint. His hips settled in the hollow of her thighs and his body moved upward, nearly fitting them together in the most basic, elemental way.

And then he paused.

"I love you, Miranda." His gaze held hers, but he didn't give her a chance to answer as he pushed deeper inside her body, claiming her in one, long, hard thrust.

She moaned as he joined their bodies, holding his gaze and digging her fingers into the hard muscle of his shoulders. Her mouth opened on a silent scream of delight as her body accepted him without qualm, knowing its mate. Reveling in the fact that they two were now One.

Then he began to move and her mind became a whirlwind of color and light, ecstasy and overall…love. Deep, abiding love tempered in passion. She could feel it with every fiber of her being. She felt it in the careful way he held her, in the way he pushed her body to its very limit and then beyond.

She buried her face in his neck, needing the scent of his skin in her nostrils, the sound of his blood swishing…echoing in her ears. She needed…

"Go ahead baby, do it. Bite me," he urged in a raspy voice that pushed her to her limits.

She licked his salty skin and found she couldn't resist. She wanted it all. With him. And only with him. She touched her elongated fangs to his neck, over the beating pulse, and then she bit down, slicing into his skin. The first drop of his blood welled and landed on her tongue, and then it happened.

She came and the floodgates in her mind crashed open. Her mind flowed into his and his into hers. She felt his momentary confusion and then the immense satisfaction he felt knowing that he really was her mate. He sent reassurance and so much love down their connection, it pushed her back up to the precipice. This time, when she came, he went with her into the abyss where only they existed. Joined. One.

How long they lingered in that nowhere land of pleasure, she wasn't sure, but she became aware again when Mag moved off her and collapsed at her side. He kept one arm around her and dragged her close to him. Apparently, he liked to snuggle after sex. She wasn't complaining one bit.

"Most shifters like to snuggle," he said, surprising her. "Get used to it." The amusement that made its way down their shared connection made her insides bubble with happiness. He'd heard her thoughts and answered them.

"Of course I did," he said, again in answer to her unspoken words. "I'm your One and you're my mate." He pulled her closer and placed a kiss on the top of her head while his breathing settled back toward its normal pace.

She turned her head to inspect the bite she'd given him. Had she remembered to seal it with her magic? Miranda was relieved to see that she had. Two red pinpricks showed on his neck, with only a tiny trace of blood. She leaned up and licked it away, loving the taste of him on her tongue.

Which made her think of other things she might want to taste that involved him. He growled and she knew he'd read her thoughts again. She was reading some pretty lascivious thoughts coming her way from his mind as well. It was all good. They were on the same page.

Miranda stalked her way down his body and staked her claim on his cock, which was already rising once more. She'd only ever been with one shifter—him. And they'd only ever made love once. She didn't know much about shifters in general, and had heard only rumors about their recovery time.

"Everything you heard is true," he boasted playfully. She felt the teasing tone of his thoughts in her mind. This sharing was going to take a little getting used to, but so far, it was fabulous.

She used the connection to learn from his thoughts exactly the way he liked her to touch him. She used her hands and her tongue, her mouth and even her teeth—very gently—to bring him to climax once more. The flavor of him was like ambrosia to her vampiric senses.

A sound came from her throat that surprised her and Mag laughed. Had she really just growled? Vampires didn't growl. At least, she'd never made such a sound before.

"This is a give and take relationship, sweetheart." Mag reached down and lifted her to lie beside him. "If you feed on my blood...and other things...you might just take on a few of my traits. Personally, I think your little growl was sexy." He kissed her lips and she caught the thought in his mind about whether or not she could shapeshift into a cougar and run with him.

"Wouldn't that be amazing?" she mused as the kiss ended and they were snuggling again. "I'd love to see the desert from your cat's point of view. I bet it's awesome."

"It is," he agreed, and she felt the satisfaction in his mind. "You know, sometimes shifters like to claw and bite during sex. Is that a problem? I mean, if I lost control and bit you, would I become a vampire too?"

She felt his concern along with the very naughty thoughts that accompanied his images of biting her while he was deep inside her. She couldn't help but respond as her body began to rev up for another round.

"It takes more than a little sip of my blood to turn someone. And I think you can feel how excited the thought of your biting me while I bite you makes me. It's the ultimate sexual thrill for one of my kind. Having sex with another vampire is rare because so few of them are willing to make themselves so vulnerable to another. There isn't a lot of trust in the bloodletter community. But a few do it because they say there's nothing like fucking and sucking at the same time."

She knew she was blushing. She wasn't one for crude language. She'd been born in a time when few women admitted to even knowing such words, much less used them, and she still hadn't quite adjusted to the modern world's casual usage of four-letter words.

"Although I'm not sure what effect a taste of my blood might have on you. It could help you heal faster. Might make you faster in general. Maybe stronger. Though you're already pretty strong and fast on your own." She loved his strength, and she knew he could feel her admiration in her thoughts. It was so amazing having the subtext of emotion behind each word they exchanged. Over time they would grow into this ability and it could become something really special.

"Do you want to give it a try?" Images of them twined together, both sporting sharp teeth sprang into his mind and fired down their connection into her brain.

"Do you have to ask?" She deliberately sent him images of them together, knowing the thoughts were firing his body back up to full speed ahead.

He rolled so that she was on top this time and helped her guide him into her body. He watched the place they were joined with glazed eyes. Somehow that made her even hotter as she began to bounce up and down over him. He helped, guiding her hips. The hard muscles in his arms flexed and moved as he assisted, his strength aiding her. She licked her lips at the sight. He really was the most beautifully built man she had ever had the good fortune to fuck. And he was all hers. For as long as they could make this last.

She banished the thought and concentrated on the man beneath her, loving the way he felt inside her. He was so deep. She felt so full of him. His cock inside her body, his mind joining with hers. The connection had blown open, but it was still new. It would take time to grow into it, she knew, and each time they made love, it would grow a little stronger.

"That's it, baby, squeeze me," he coached in a low, sexy voice that made her insides clench on him. He sucked in air as she moaned and swayed above him.

And then it was time. She couldn't hold out much longer. She needed to taste his essence, to have her aching fangs sink into him and take his blood inside her body, into her spirit. To join them on the deepest, most elemental level. She crept forward, lowering herself over his chest, altering the angle of penetration and ratcheting her excitement higher. His cock hit a secret little spot inside her that made her want to scream with delight every time it rubbed in just the right way.

She licked a path along his neck, looking for just the right spot as his body surged into hers again, touching that spot that sent what felt like joyous jolts of electricity through her nervous system. One more ought to do it. She didn't want to wait.

Miranda bit him and felt an answering bite on her shoulder, just where it joined her neck as he thrust deep, one last time. She exploded, feeling him do the same. He growled in his chest, sending off little shockwaves against her nipples which only made her rocket higher into oblivion.

He'd done this to her. Mag and Mag alone could make her see the stars without ever leaving the Earth.

They had a few hours left until dawn, and they spent them in each other's arms. They made love repeatedly, learning the new connections between their minds. Though they couldn't always hear each other's thoughts in words, Miranda said that would come in time. He did pick up on her emotions and the sensations coming from her were pretty amazing. He gained a whole new understanding of pleasure—and of what made her hot. He looked forward to trying out their new ability in other settings too.

Miranda was taking the lead on the mental stuff while Mag was in charge of her pleasure and all physical comforts. He ran a bath in the giant Jacuzzi tub for them both, then made love to her in the water, and then again on the vanity—

sidetracked while he was trying to dry off her luscious body.

When dawn broke, she fell asleep in his arms. He stayed with her for about an hour, just looking at her and marveling at how greatly he had been blessed. To find his mate and have her be such a caring, loving soul… His joy was beyond comprehension or explanation.

Finally though, he rose from the bed and started his day. He had a few things to do and wheels to set in motion before he grabbed a cat nap this afternoon. He wanted to be there when she woke in his bed. He especially wanted to make love to her again before they faced whatever the night would bring.

If he was a betting man, he'd expect that promised summons from the Master vampire to be waiting for them as soon as night fell.

CHAPTER NINE

Mag wasn't surprised when he got the message later in the afternoon. It was just before dusk when he checked his voice mail. All through Miranda's recuperation, he'd managed to keep up with his paperwork for Redstone Construction, working remotely from his home office. Apparently the Master had been unable to find out where Mag had taken Miranda, and had resorted to tracking down his work number.

Nice.

The message wasn't from the Master himself, but from one of his servants. He kept a few humans employed in his place of business. He was even rumored to have a tame mage he used for daytime missions that required knowledge of the supernatural world. The humans were kept strictly in the dark about the Master's true nature. They just thought he was an eccentric club owner who partied all night while they ran the day-to-day business. Tony's vampire magic made sure they kept believing it. He could influence their minds at will, and make them believe just about anything he wanted. Vampires at his level had skills that were kind of scary, but they didn't have much impact on shifter minds.

For that, Mag was grateful. He listened to the message with surprise. It was very polite and carefully worded. Mag and his *plus one* were invited to a soiree at the Master's penthouse on top of his luxury hotel on the Strip.

The building was nice. Not up to Redstone Construction standards of course, but nice all the same, Mag thought, as they rode up to the penthouse in the express elevator. Miranda elbowed him. She'd been picking up on the flavor of his thoughts at random moments, and he felt her amusement at his prideful musings.

They'd agreed to keep the connection loose for now. She was able to control it a lot better than him, seeing as how she had more practice with the psychic gifts she'd gained when she'd become immortal. He was learning, but she was definitely more in control of the connection between their minds than he was at the moment.

He was cool with that. For now. He'd figure it out eventually. After all, they would have their whole lives together to work on it if he had anything to say about it.

The door whooshed open at the top floor and they were met by sounds of elegant music being played by a string quartet. Men and women lounged here and there with full glasses of wine. Some were eating from the buffet, which meant this was a mixed gathering of vampires and humans. Mag would be on his guard. He sniffed discretely and noted each scent. Not a single shifter of any kind was in the big penthouse suite.

That didn't mean Mag was totally on his own here. He'd made contingency plans. His older brothers had taught him well—and pledged their help. Mag had taken them up on the offer, and if trouble arose here tonight, there was backup standing by.

A sleek vampire came toward them. The woman was an icy blond and though she smiled, it did not reach her eyes.

"Miranda, darling, so good to see you again."

The woman gave Miranda the society air kiss that made Mag want to laugh, but he didn't dare. It wouldn't do to insult a vamp in the Master's lair. Mag felt Miranda's reaction to the woman. She wanted to roll her eyes, which pretty much matched Mag's impulses. Mag sensed there was no love lost between the two women. The emotions he was gleaning from Miranda indicated a complicated relationship existed between the two females.

"Cassandra, this is Magnus Redstone. Mag, this is my sister, Cassie." Mag interpreted the flavor of her words along with the mixed emotions to mean something very different than he would have thought when she used the word *sister*. Mag felt the nuances now. Miranda wanted him to stay on his toes. He sent her reassuring thoughts through their link. He wouldn't let his guard down. Not for one minute.

He shook hands with the lovely vampire, noting that she had none of the warmth or openness in her expression that made Miranda the true beauty of their weird little family. Cassandra also squeezed his hand a little too tight. He was sure it was some kind of one-upmanship display to remind him that she may look fragile, but she was far from it. No worries. He wouldn't forget.

"Tony's waiting for you," Cassandra said, letting go of Mag's slightly bruised hand. Without waiting for an answer, she turned, apparently expecting them to follow. That she used the Master's nickname was not lost on Mag.

They followed her to a private room where the Master Vampire was holding court. At least that's what it looked like. Mag had never seen anything like it, though he'd been introduced to the Master a time or two before. It was well understood that the Redstone Clan was the strongest group of Others in the area, therefore the Clan Alpha was top cat in Las Vegas.

Grif kept an open dialog with the Master, and the two groups occasionally shared information. For example, they talked contingencies when there was a shared threat. Grif was in charge of those kinds of discussions, and Mag knew he was cautious about bloodletters. But Mag also knew that Grif had an overall positive impression of the Master. Mag hoped his brother was right and this guy was okay.

When he saw them standing just inside the doorway, Antoine de Latourette, known to his close associates as Tony, stood and motioned for the room to clear. Mag wasn't sure what to make of the somewhat imperious action. He was having a hard time getting a read on the Master. This meeting could still go either way.

The room emptied quickly, leaving only Tony and Cassandra facing Mag and Miranda. For a moment, nobody spoke. Finally, the Master broke his silence.

"It's good to see you whole, young Miranda." He smiled and Mag almost believed the expression on the Master's face this time. Then those piercing eyes turned on Mag. "I understand we have you and your family to thank for finding her."

"I'm not sure how much Grif told you." A polite lie. Mag knew what his brother had shared with the Master vampire. Not the entire story, but everything about how they'd found Miranda on that raid months ago. "Miranda was being held captive by one of the mages that murdered my mother. She was near death. Starved for blood. She had been cut repeatedly, drained of her blood and her magic over a period of months."

Tony's eyes seemed to hold compassion when he turned back to look at Miranda, but Mag couldn't be sure. Grif had told him this guy was over seven hundred years old. He was probably a better actor than most to have hidden within human society for so long.

"You've been through an ordeal most of us would not survive." The Master seemed to look at her with new respect. "But I am surprised no one was killed during your initial release."

"I slashed the panther," she mumbled, as if ashamed. "I have apologized to him and his mate, but I have not been able to forget the blind rage that drove me to hurt him so badly," she admitted under the pressure of the Master's gaze.

"The panther?" the Master's brows drew together in question.

"She means Slade. Our priestess's mate," Mag helped clarify.

"You took down the snowcat?" Even more respect filled the Master's eyes as he looked at Miranda.

Mag also realized the Master knew a lot more about Slade than they'd thought. Slade's dual nature—black panther and Himalayan snowcat—was something he kept under wraps, for the most part. It wasn't normal for a shifter to share his soul with two creatures, but then, nothing about the mythical, highly magical snowcat followed normal rules. The Master must have pretty good intel sources if he knew about Slade.

"It was a lucky shot, but still, enough to damage him," Mag admitted, not sure how much to say. He didn't want to give away any more information much about Slade's rather surprising vulnerability to Miranda's attack, but he also didn't want to detract from Miranda's strength. He had to balance his words just right.

"Interesting. But what made her stop?" The Master was talking directly to Mag again, which was fine with him. He'd spare Miranda the interrogation if he could.

"I did. I arrived just as she was about to bite him and saw her. I called her name and she stopped." Mag remembered the moment when he'd seen her again for the first time in over two years. She'd been about ready to savage Slade, and the memory of the state she'd been in still broke his heart. She'd been so weak. So fragile both mentally and physically. So close to the point of no return.

"Ah yes. You two knew each other before. Tell me, was it a long affair? I assume it was. She's stronger than she should be for her age. I can only assume it was your blood that made her that way." The accusation was aimed at Mag and he bristled. The cat inside him wanted to scratch and claw, but he repressed the urge.

"If you must know, it was a one-night thing. She was gone when I woke up, and I never saw her again until that night in the mage's lair. Before that night she'd only had one hit of my blood."

"And since?" Tony demanded harshly.

"Yes," Miranda stepped in, answering the question. "On the night they found me."

"And nothing since? I find that hard to believe." Tony scoffed at her answer.

Mag felt Miranda's anger rising and he thought it was about time. He tried to send cautionary feelings along their bond, hoping she would choose her words wisely.

"Last night, we renewed our bond. Master, I must report to you that I have found my One." Her tone was strong and sure, her gaze direct.

"It's forbidden!" Cassandra gasped and then fell silent. You could have heard a pin drop while the Master examined them. And then he sighed heavily.

"Do you feel the same?" the Master asked Mag in an almost weary voice.

"Miranda is my mate. I knew that the moment I met her more than two years ago. I won't let her go a second time." Mag stood firm against the Master's banked intensity.

"You two present a real problem for me," Tony said at last, steepling his fingers as he sat in his high-backed chair.

"But Master," Cassandra piped in, "this cannot be allowed! It's forbidden!"

"Actually, it's not," Tony drawled, not even looking at the blond woman. "I've seen such unions before." He looked at Miranda and then Mag. "But the paths of such couples were never easy."

"We're prepared to face whatever comes," Mag replied immediately, standing firm.

"You may think you are," Tony allowed. "And I have no doubt that you are every bit as tough as your brothers, Magnus. I have respect for them and your Clan. But you cannot know the trials ahead, and your mate is still very young for a bloodletter. She may not be up to the challenge. In which case, you will both fall."

Mag could feel Miranda bristling at his side. She didn't like the Master's low opinion of her. Not one bit.

"I may be young, but I've been through hell and back, and not one of your precious minions even cared to look for me." Miranda let loose with both barrels while Mag silently applauded. "My dear *sister*," she practically sneered the word, "didn't even bother to notice I was gone."

"Oh, I noticed," Cassandra said, and not in a friendly way. It was clear the other woman had probably wanted Miranda dead for a long time. Mag took note, filing away that information for later consideration. For now, he was on guard, watching every detail.

"And did nothing," Miranda continued, her voice condemning. "I would have died but for Mag. He is my family now. I would renounce you if I could, Cassandra."

"Now, now, ladies." Tony watched the animosity between the women with something that looked like mild interest to Mag. Then again, the old guy probably had complete control over his facial expressions after so many centuries. Nothing would show that he didn't want to show. "You will be civil to one another in my home. Cassie, darling, would you go and fetch a bottle of my favorite? There's a good girl." Tony sent the blond off on his errand, clearly wanting her out of the room. Cassie's expression could have melted steel, but she followed orders and stomped out of the room.

As soon as the door closed behind her, Tony gestured for them to sit. Mag saw the mask of indifference slide of the Master's face as he leaned forward in his chair. Finally, he thought, they were seeing the real man beneath the carefully controlled expressions.

"She won't come back for at least ten minutes," Tony said. "Enough time for us to speak freely. Miranda, I am truly sorry nobody searched for you. I had assumed Cassie was taking care of her family, but I have learned since your disappearance how wrong I was about her. You were covering for her all these years, weren't you?"

Miranda nodded slowly. "For a long time, I blamed myself for the way she is," she admitted. "But during my captivity, I had a lot of time to think. I didn't do anything wrong. Our maker was a cruel and selfish man. If anyone's to blame, it's him." Mag saw a little hint of Miranda's memories of a handsome vampire through their connection, but he was missing a big chunk of the story, he was sure.

"Geoff was a fool," Tony admitted. "He got what was coming to him and you are not to blame. Everyone but Cassie knows it."

"She still blames me for his death. She has from the very beginning."

"I did not realize the depths of her cruelty until recent events, Miranda. I'm sorry to have been so blind where your family was concerned."

An apology from the Master Vampire? Mag was impressed.

"Miranda will explain the delicate details about her family to you later, I'm sure," Tony added when he noticed Mag's curious expression. "For now, I will give you my blessing, for what it's worth, on your union. I ask only that you don't publicize it. I fear that with so many shifters in Las Vegas, and so many youngsters looking to increase their power, if it became known openly that you two are mated, the less scrupulous of my people would begin to prey on yours, Magnus. That is something neither of us want. So for everyone's sake, you must keep your union as low profile as possible. To that end, I'm creating a new position within my power structure. For the first time, both bloodletters and shifters are going to have liaisons. Liaisons that will have to work very closely together."

Mag smiled. It was an elegant solution to the problem. Tony was right. If their mating was common knowledge, it would be open season on shifter blood, and nobody wanted that.

"You, Magnus, are now the official shifter liaison to my court. I've talked it over with Grif and he agrees, though you will undoubtedly talk to him about it after we're done here." Tony nodded as if he expected no less. "The position will give you an excuse to be in constant contact with my own liaison, Miranda."

"Do you think it'll work?" Miranda asked, looking from Mag to Tony and back again.

"Yeah, I think it just might." Mag smiled, glad his brother and the Master had been plotting behind his back. They'd come up with a good option for everyone concerned.

"Cassie might be a problem," Miranda put in.

"She is already a problem," Tony agreed. "I am having her watched. As soon as she returns, I will compel her to secrecy about your union."

Mag knew the Master was the most powerful vampire in the city. He probably had the skill with magic, and strength behind it after seven centuries of practice, to bind the younger vamp. Mag didn't care to speculate on what Tony could do to just about anyone, if he felt the desire to screw with their minds. Luckily, the priestess had assured Grif—and by extension, the rest of the family—that Tony was on their side. He wasn't capricious or evil, for which everyone in a hundred mile radius could be thankful.

"Cassandra has been angling for more and more power within my domain," Tony went on. "She fancies herself my right hand. I've allowed it so that I can keep a close eye on her, but the time is coming when she will overstep her bounds and I will have to call her to task. Leave her to me for now. I will keep her on a short leash."

They left the penthouse a short while later. They'd settled things for now, but Miranda still worried about Cassandra. She was devious. Even the Master probably didn't realize the depths of her cunning. Miranda would have to be on guard. And she'd have to tell Mag the whole, sordid story so he understood the situation fully.

She wasn't looking forward to it. They kept silent until they were heading home in Mag's car. He'd taken the precaution of having it guarded by two shifters while they were at the party. No one had gotten near enough to plant any sort of tracker on it this time.

Before they'd left, the Master had explained that as his new liaison, Miranda had moved significantly up in the bloodletter hierarchy. She reported only to him now, and if any bloodletter interfered with her in any way—and surveillance would definitely be considered interference—there would be severe consequences.

Miranda hadn't looked for any sort of increase in position within the vampire community, but it had come to her nonetheless. Though it would take some getting used to, the advantages to her new role far outweighed any disadvantage, from what she could see. Things just might work out after all. And if she had to keep quiet about finding her One, then so be it. She didn't exactly have a ton of friends among her people. In fact, she had damn few.

Mag reached across the seat and took her hand in his. She realized he was picking up on her emotions and maybe some of her thoughts as well. The connection between them was strong, but they hadn't yet really shared their thoughts in words. That would come in time. For now, they had to learn their way...together.

"It'll be harder to hide our mating from my people than yours," Mag said into the silence. "But if it keeps you safe, I'll do anything."

"You know I feel the same." She squeezed his hand. "Whatever we need to do to be together, that's what we'll do." She felt good putting the feelings she knew they shared into words. "Now..." She really wasn't looking forward to what she had to do next. "There are a few things you need to know about my past."

She knew he sensed her dread. She felt his emotions through their connection, and was pleased that he didn't want to put her through dredging up the past. She, on the other hand, felt it had to be done. Her past had to be put out in the open so nothing could surprise him later. She took a deep breath.

"I didn't become...what I am...by choice," she began. "My maker, Geoffry, was a predator of the worst kind. He was young for a bloodletter, with only a century or two under his belt. He decided he wanted a harem of playmates and began turning women against their will. At first, he chose pretty prostitutes. Cassandra is the only one of those many women who continues to exist. She was one of the few who were happy of the change when she woke up from a night of debauchery to find herself immortal. The others weren't quite so strong of will. A few ran out into the sun on their first day as immortals. Others fell to different circumstances. Regardless, when Geoff got tired of playing with women of questionable virtue, he began looking around for others. Somehow I caught his eye and he began the seduction."

She felt so stupid, even now, all these years later. "I was innocent. Naïve." She looked out the window at the passing scenery. The desert was really beautiful at night, but nothing could quell the ugly memories of her past. "Geoff began to court me and I thought I was the luckiest girl in the world to have such an elegant and educated suitor. He took me out dancing and to parties. He was so worldly and I was such a little girl back then. Inevitably, I fell for his act and on the night I expected him to propose marriage, he attacked and drained me almost to death. He gave me a huge dose of his blood and the change began. I woke up a day later as I am now."

She had to pause to regain control of her emotions before she could go on with her story. She blinked several times to halt the tears she could feel welling in her eyes.

"I couldn't go back to my family. Geoff had arranged everything. He faked my death so my family wouldn't look for me. He whisked me away from everything I knew. I was totally dependent on him for everything. Cassandra was my tormentor from day one. She didn't like being replaced by a younger model, and she hated the fact that I was a virtuous woman. She harassed me constantly, belittling the fact that even after all I'd been through, I was still a virgin. Geoff took care of that though. I'd barely recovered my strength when he used his magic to seduce me into his bed." She felt the old bitterness and disgust at her maker's actions fill her mind.

"If he wasn't already dead, I'd kill him for you," Mag said in a quiet, deadly growl at her side.

It was just what she needed to hear to anchor her back to the here and now instead of the miserable past she'd already survived. Dwelling on Geoff's treachery did her no good. She'd been there, done that for far too long, and didn't want to go back.

"Cassie blames me for his death. She's probably right. I ran from him and he was stupid enough to chase me. He got caught out in the sun and fried. And I was glad." She reveled the feeling of bitter satisfaction she'd felt when she woke the next night, knowing he was dead. "There's a special bond between us and our makers. I didn't know how, but I knew the next time I woke that the bond was severed. He was gone. And I cried in relief. And I ran. I knew the remaining members of his harem would be after me. They'd want revenge. Without him, they'd actually have to work for a living and scramble to figure out how to get by. Most of them only had their looks to fall back on and not much in the brain department. He mostly picked weak-willed women. Almost all were dead before the next year was out. I felt it each time one of them left this realm. The bond between us faded each time one did something stupid and died the final death. The sibling bond isn't quite as strong as the bond to the maker, but it's still there."

"How did you meet up with Cassandra again?" Mag asked, calmer now.

"We only reunited a few years ago when I moved to Las Vegas. She was already here, which made sense to me. She was always one for glitter without much substance. This city is perfect for her. It was a tough reunion. She actually dragged me before the Master demanding justice for the death of our maker. The Master stopped just shy of laughing in her face once he heard the whole story. Besides Cassie, and now you, he's the only one who knows how my maker died. Though I've long suspected Cassie was spreading lies about me. I wasn't welcomed by many, and those who did give me the benefit of the doubt were cautious. I didn't mind because I didn't choose this life and I don't particularly like hanging out with other vampires. I go my own way."

"And that's just one of the things I love about you."

"If I were a shifter, I guess I'd be a lone wolf, eh?" She tried for a joke.

Mag laughed outright and she was glad she'd managed to lighten the mood. "Honey, you're mated to a cougar shifter. You could never been a mangy mutt." He reached over and stroked her hair. She felt the love coming from him through their connection and in his actions. How had she ever been so blessed as to have this amazing man in her life? "And actually, I understand all about wanting to roam alone at times. Ask any of my brothers. We've all taken time here and there to go out and be on our own. Cats are probably the most independent of all shifters."

"And yet your family has built up a huge community. It seems like a contradiction."

"Sweetheart, you still don't get it. We're *cats*. We are *made* of contradiction." He chuckled and she joined in, glad to have something to make them both smile after the chaos of the evening.

CHAPTER TEN

While Mag and Miranda played house, Cassie was plotting. She'd been having sex with Raintree off and on for years. They were well matched, she and the Master's second-in-command. Neither trusted the other and both liked to live on the edge.

The fact that either could turn on the other at any time added spice to the sex and there was nothing like fucking and sucking at the same time. That's why, every few months, they hooked up to have a bit of vampire nookie. Sometimes alone. Sometimes with a few humans around who liked to be subjugated. Either way, fucking Raintree was some of the hottest sex she'd ever had.

And Cassie had fucked her way through the centuries. She'd become a whore because she liked sex. A lot. In modern times, they'd probably have called her a nymphomaniac, but Cassie didn't care. She liked sex and the power it gave her over men. Always had.

"I don't like the way my *sister*," Cassie sneered the last word, "has jumped up in the hierarchy. She doesn't deserve it and she shouldn't be allowed to drink from her pet shifter. It's not right."

"Maybe so," Raintree said, his voice lazy after climax as he reclined in the huge bed he kept in his underground lair. "But what are you going to do about it?"

Cassie didn't like the rhetorical question. Raintree had clearly not thought this through. There was opportunity in this adversity and Cassie was just the vampiress to take advantage—if she could round up some more highly-placed, higher-powered support. She couldn't do this on her own, but she could definitely reap the rewards of talking some bigger, stronger vamps into doing it for her.

She finished pouring the wine and returned to the bed, handing Raintree a full glass while she sipped at her own, fondling him with her spare hand. Men were so easy to manipulate. Get a hand on their joystick and you could maneuver them into any position you wanted.

"I don't think I'm the only one to think Tony's gone too far this time," she purred, stroking Raintree expertly. "I bet, with not too much convincing, we could gather more than a few supporters and replace him." She spelled it out, sitting up and straddling Raintree. "*You* could replace him. You're strong enough. Ambitious enough. Don't tell me you haven't thought about challenging him for the role of Master."

Raintree's eyes narrowed as he guided her hips. He slid into her as she began a lazy movement on his cock. She let him believe he was in control, though she really held all the power. Men liked it that way and she saw no reason to shatter their little illusions. Not if it got her what she wanted.

"I've thought about it." His voice was lazy with sensual overload. They'd been at it for hours already—long enough to take the edge off.

"I would pledge my loyalty to you, Aramis. So would a number of others I've been talking to. Not everyone is on board with Tony's weak approach to shifters and the Others in this town. We should rule the night, and those who walk the day should tremble in fear for the time we wake. Taking a back seat to the Redstones and their pathetic Clan isn't the way it should be. We are stronger. Smarter. We've always been superior to those mongrel cats and dogs. We are the masters. Not them."

She punctuated her words with expert rolls of her hips that brought them both a great deal of pleasure. She could ride Raintree for hours. That was one of the benefits of screwing her own kind. Humans just didn't have the staying power.

"What do you want in return for your support?" Raintree asked astutely. He knew her well enough to realize she wouldn't stick her neck out for free. Cassandra never did anything for free. She was a whore to the heart.

"A spot on your council, and the pleasure of killing my little sister and her pet." She wanted more of course, but that was enough to start with.

"Why not?" Raintree almost appeared to shrug, but the cunning in his eyes belied the gesture. "We'll start tomorrow night. Gather your forces and I'll make a few calls. We'll meet at my club at midnight. First we'll take out your sister and the cat, then we'll see about Tony."

Damn. He could be decisive when he wanted. She liked that about him. He might seem lazy and urbane, but underneath he was every bit the scrappy fighter she was.

Raintree guided her hips, moving them faster and she complied. Talk was over for now. She'd planted the seed and he would make it grow...with her guidance. She was very good at guiding men. Leading them around by the nose—or other body parts. It's what she did best.

And when all was said and done, Cassie's wretched little sister would learn once and for all that hell hath no fury like a whore denied her sugar daddy. Cassie would finally make the bitch pay for killing their maker.

Miranda and Mag stayed in the house he'd built in the desert for another couple of weeks without much input from the outside world. At least, Miranda didn't interact with anyone but Mag. She slept a lot, but regained her strength at record pace with Mag feeding her senses both physically and magically. Their bond grew stronger each time they made love and with each moment they spent together, simply being.

She cherished their time together, knowing things would change sooner or later. They always did. And not usually for the better, in her experience.

Miranda spent her nights with Mag, able to stay up longer and longer until finally, she felt back to her old self. In fact, she was much stronger than she had been, and would probably grow stronger still as their relationship deepened. She knew Mag spent part of the daylight hours working remotely, able to perform his duties for the construction company via the computer and phone connections built into his state of the art home.

Their home, now. She had the Master's blessing and that's all she needed to accept Mag's mate claim. She wasn't a hundred percent sure what shifter mating entailed, but she figured at some point they'd get his family's official blessing on their union…or not. Whatever happened, they would face it together.

Along about the end of the week, Mag came to greet her when she woke at dusk, as he usually did. Sometimes they made love. Sometimes they just cuddled. This night, he handed her a glass of wine as he sat beside her in bed, sipping from his own glass. Apparently he wanted to talk. She eyed him over the rim of her goblet with a bit of trepidation.

Unless forced to discuss more weighty matters, he'd kept all conversations to light subjects that he thought wouldn't upset her. When she pressed him on his ability to tiptoe around the more serious things they needed to talk about, he admitted he didn't want anything to interfere with her full recovery. Not anxiety, or any kind of worry about things that could wait until she was all better.

Now that she *was* better…well…she assumed now was the time to broach the tougher subjects they'd been ignoring for a while. She wasn't really looking forward to it.

"My brother Grif is hosting a get-together at his place on Saturday night. He invited us specially and I think he wants to introduce the concept of you being the vampire liaison to some of the more highly ranked members of the Clan."

Miranda was surprised by the invitation, but intrigued.

"How do you think that's going to go over?" She frowned, thinking over the possibilities. Some of the echoes of thought she picked up from Mag's mind mirrored her own anxiety.

"Honestly, I have no idea." He sighed heavily, crossing his ankles. He was stretched out beside her in their bed, his back against the headboard, his jean-clad legs flowing down the length of the bed, on top of the comforter. "Matt will be the most receptive, of course. I checked, and he'll be at the gathering. The rest of my family will probably be cautious but welcoming. Grif set up the liaison thing with Tony, after all. He's dealt with vamps before and is open minded. I'm not sure about the other Alphas."

"How many will be there?"

She knew the Redstone Clan as a whole was structured around a core group of Alphas of each species who represented all the shifters who came under their rule. There was a werewolf Alpha who spoke for all the wolves, a raptor Alpha, a bear Alpha, and so on. It sounded like the leaders of each group would be at this little shindig and Miranda swallowed hard, a little bit of panic rising at the thought of having to face so much potential disapproval.

"More than a few. Plus their mates, though not all of them are mated. It's going to be a backyard barbeque with an informal Clan meeting beforehand, and probably a bit of a howl after."

"What's a howl, exactly?" She thought she knew, but she wanted a more detailed explanation than the images she picked up from his thoughts.

"Howls can take different forms. Sometimes they're mate hunts. Sometimes it's just a group of shifters taking their animal forms and running through the woods. There may or may not be some hunting involved, but nothing dangerous. Most of the time, it's all in good fun. Especially in our Clan. Grif has made sure we have more civilized ways to handle most disputes than challenge fights and dirty tricks." He took a sip of his wine. "We don't have to stay for the run if you don't want to."

"But it sure would impress everyone if I could shapeshift into a cougar and join you." She finished his unspoken thought, smiling when he looked affronted.

Sometimes his thoughts came to her so clearly, it was hard to resist tweaking him a bit. Of the two of them, she was much more comfortable in sharing their thoughts and looked forward to the future when they'd perfected their bond and could speak in words, mind to mind. He was more resistant, which was probably why they hadn't yet manifested the ability.

"Can you?" He almost seemed to hold his breath in anticipation of her answer.

She tilted her head, considering. "I'm not really sure. I've never tried to do a cougar. I can do monsters and a very convincing baby bear, but I don't think that would inspire the right kind of memories—especially for Slade and the priestess." She could almost laugh about it now, but she still regretted attacking the panther shifter when he and his mate had freed her.

"Yeah, we probably don't want to remind anybody of that night. But if you could become a sweet little female cougar, I think they'd be a little more receptive to you. Plus, I'd love it. I always dreamed of running through the forest alongside my mate, chasing her tail."

She laughed as he leered, and right then and there she decided to try. She drained the glass of the last sips of wine and placed it on the bedside table before turning back to give him a smacking kiss. She evaded his arms when he would have drawn her in for more and bounded off the bed. He grinned when she stood before him, but she didn't think he picked up on her plans for the next few moments until she called her magic and started to shift.

She thought of the beautiful cougar he became and pictured a feminine version of the same. Sleeker, a bit smaller, and more compact, but tawny and four-legged with a long tail. She felt herself compressing and expanding into the form of the cat in her mind and a moment later, she was looking up at the bed through cat's eyes from a much lower position.

Experimentally, she waggled her tail in Mag's direction and he chuckled. The look of admiration in his eyes was worth every moment of effort on her part, though truth be told, it hadn't taxed her much at all to become the cougar. Dining on his shifter blood had made her stronger than she'd ever been, and her magic had flowed her essence into the cat's form with very little effort.

She padded over to him and reached up with her front paws as he swung his legs over the side of the bed and sat on the edge. Her paws were on either side of his muscular thighs as he reached out and scratched her behind the ears. Man, oh man, that felt *good*.

A rumbling noise started in her chest and she realized she was purring. Mag's eyes widened before a satisfied smile lit his face.

"You're gorgeous, sweetheart. They're going to love you as much as I do."

On Saturday night, Mag was a bit more nervous than he liked. This was his family. He should be able to count on their support. Instead, he worried that they'd reject his mate—rejecting him in the process. He'd never been in such a position before, but he knew if he had to make a choice, he'd chose Miranda every time. His mate was even more important to him than his family, which was really saying something.

They dressed casually, yet he knew Miranda took extra pains with her appearance. He knew from the incredible communication they shared that she wanted to make a good impression. She didn't want to shame him in front of his family. Catching that thought, he went over and wrapped his arms around her, kissing her hair.

"You are too good for me, Miranda." It was a thought he had often, wondering how he'd been so blessed as to have a mate as amazing at her. Miranda was everything to him. She was the brightest light in his world.

She turned in his arms and hugged him tight. "Whatever happens tonight, we will always have each other, right?"

"Without a doubt. You know how I feel, right? My family is great and I love them, but you are the most important person in my life now, sweetheart. Nothing will come between me and my mate. Not even well-meaning but misguided family." He sighed. "Of course, I'm probably worrying for nothing. They were pretty cool about us at that little intervention they staged." He chuckled now at the memory. "But I guess I'm concerned about the rest of the Alphas from the Clan. Some really hate bloodletters. If they cause waves, it could be uncomfortable for us."

"We'll deal," she said, pulling out of his arms. She took one last look in the mirror and turned to walk out of the bedroom with him. He put his arm around her and didn't let go until they were out of the house and in the garage.

He kissed her soundly before opening the passenger door of his Lamborghini. He wanted to zip through the desert night tonight, opting for the fastest car he owned. Mag really liked cars. Most of the Redstone brothers did, and they had quite a collection between them, now that the company could easily support such extravagances. Each year, he bought something new with the bonus money he earned from contracts completed on-time or even early, in some cases. The harder he worked, the more money he made to play with.

They were on the highway, heading toward Clan lands when he confirmed his suspicions about exactly who was acting as escort for them tonight. He caught sight of a raptor in the air above them—and not just any raptor. This was the Alpha of the group. The biggest badass of the feathered fliers.

"Looks like we might have an unexpected ally," he muttered as the bird allowed itself to be seen for a moment.

"The owl, you mean? He's one of yours, right?" Miranda asked, scanning the sky out her window.

"Mine? I wouldn't say that." Mag had to chuckle. "He's a shifter, but he doesn't really answer to anyone except Grif. That owl is the Alpha of *all* the birds under our Clan's banner. Not just owls. He's the top bird of them all, and I haven't seen him in a while. If he's our escort tonight, that means something."

"What exactly does it mean?" she whispered, still trying to catch another glimpse of the elusive owl that shadowed their path.

"I won't know for certain until we get to the meeting, but I'm going to take it as a positive sign. Joe's not strictly a member of the security team. Although a few of his raptors have been working for my brother Steve and helping guard our house, Joe's been flying under the radar—until about five minutes ago."

"Why would he show himself now?"

"Who really knows? The guy is downright inscrutable sometimes. But if he volunteered to see us to our destination safely, then I have to think maybe it's a vote in our favor. The owls, being true night hunters, have a bit more interaction with vampires than other shifters."

"What kind of owl is he?"

"Horny," Mag replied, the joke something he and his brothers had often sniggered over. "Although I guess the proper name is *great horned* owl. But the other name fits. Our boy Joe does seem to attract the ladies."

"So he's unmated?"

"Yeah," Mag answered cautiously. He didn't get any alarming vibes through their connection, but jealousy wasn't something that was rational. She no doubt picked up on his feelings because a second later, her hand covered his on the console between them.

"I was just wondering if he'd understand the mating imperative. If maybe that was why he might be sympathetic to us."

"To be honest, I don't know much about him on a personal level. I don't interact with him much and he's even more private than most shifters. Grif knows him best, of course. Grif knows all the Alphas that answer to him. Next to Grif, I guess Steve is probably the other one of my brothers who has close dealings with Joe because so many of his fliers take shifts in security. Having so many raptors in our Clan gives us a real advantage when it comes to the business. First, they love working at height and are super safe to have as iron workers on our tallest projects, but they also are great at covert security. They always have the high ground and most of them can pass for ordinary birds of prey, even if they are a little bigger than their wild counterparts. Joe though, he's the biggest of them all. A human sees him in flight and they're gonna wonder at his size. Luckily, his beast is nocturnal and very well camouflaged. Few humans will ever catch sight of him in the air at night."

"So for bird shifters, what you're saying is that size really does matter?" She smirked and he had to laugh with her. He loved his mate's irreverent sense of humor. Hell, he loved everything about her.

They didn't have time for more conversation because at that moment, he pulled up in front of the old family homestead. While he hadn't grown up in this house, he'd lived there while his mother was alive. In fact, she'd been murdered in the back garden she'd loved so much. They'd had her ceremony there as well—the one that had sent her body to dust and her spirit into the next realm.

There were a lot of memories in that house. Good memories and some bad. Lots of happy times and some of the most difficult days of his life. His mother's death had impacted them all in different ways. Mag had taken it hard— as had all his brothers.

Their little sister—the only surviving female of their bloodline—had taken it hardest of all. Grif was working with her, as was the priestess, to lessen the trauma. Poor little Belinda had been the one to find their mother's body and it had left her scarred emotionally.

Grif was the best with Belinda. He had been more of a

father figure to her than an older brother for a long time. They'd lost their dad years ago, when Belinda was just a baby. Grif had stepped up and more or less raised her. He'd been her big brother and her Alpha all wrapped up in one, which wasn't the normal order of things. But it worked for them.

Mag couldn't even imagine what the poor kid had gone through when she'd found their mother's body, but he'd done his best to be supportive, in his way. Mag was the quiet one of the family, but he'd held Belinda while she cried and been there for her when the rest of the family went off, running around trying to catch the bad guys without much direction.

After Slade had shown up and organized them a bit, Mag had been able to join the hunting parties. Belinda had been left with their cousin and his mate, who were wonderful with her, and the brothers had done their part in hunting down the perpetrators. It was at the beginning of that hunt that he'd found Miranda.

Since then, he'd been very distant from his family. It pained him to have to do it, but his mate had to come first. Tonight would be key in deciding their future. Would he have to cut ties with the Clan and keep the chasm between himself and his immediate family, or would they find a way to move forward together into a new, closer relationship that included his mate? Mag was nervous to see how it would all turn out.

He pulled up to the house and Mag got out of the Lamborghini. He moved around the car to Miranda's door, taking a deep breath, still wondering how this evening would turn out. Miranda got out and stepped right into his arms. He'd almost forgotten how easily she could read him now. Although they weren't communicating in words through their connection—though she assured him that was something that would come in time—they definitely felt each other's emotions.

Miranda hugged him, reaching up to place little kisses on his cheek and jaw. "I love you, my One. I wish I could ease your worry."

"You do, Miranda. Just by being here, you make life worth living." He whispered, not even realizing how deeply he meant the words until they were uttered into the darkness of the night around them.

"Come on, you two. You're the last to arrive." A voice came to them from out of the darkness and Mag looked up to see Joe walking toward them in his human form. He was buttoning a shirt he'd retrieved from somewhere. Shifters had to plan ahead so they didn't end up bare-assed naked all the time. Apparently the owl was a planner and Mag had to approve. He looked as if he'd just stepped out of some fancy fashion ad or something. No doubt about it, the owl was a snazzy dresser.

Mag reluctantly released Miranda, turning to face the newcomer with her at his side. He had to be polite. While they were both Alpha, Mag was third in command of the entire Clan while Joe was the leader of all the bird shifters in the Clan. They'd never actually figured out where that put them personally. Which was higher ranked? It was hard to say.

But tonight of all nights, Mag didn't want any conflict. Or at least, any more conflict than he already expected. If Joe was offering the hand of peace, Mag would take it. Gladly.

"Joseph Nightwing, may I introduce Miranda van Allyn. Miranda, this is Joseph, Alpha of the fliers in our Clan." Mag had to hold back his beast's instincts to protect his mate. The cat didn't like watching her touch the other man, even to shake hands. Thankfully, it was a brief handshake and Joe stepped back right away, seeming to understand.

"I wanted to meet you before the gathering," Joe declared, speaking directly to Miranda, surprising Mag a bit. "I've had good dealings with your Master. In fact, I spoke with him about your situation yesterday and he convinced me to give you my support—or at least reserve judgment until I'd met you and learned more about you."

Mag knew Miranda was a little taken aback by Joe's words, but she hid it well. She gave him a tentative smile and nodded. "Thank you for being open minded," she replied cautiously. Miranda was good at being diplomatic when necessary.

Joe seemed to like her answer, nodding again and stepping back. The front door had opened and Mag saw his brother Bob looking out at them.

"Guess we'd better head inside," Mag said and the three of them began walking up the path toward the door.

CHAPTER ELEVEN

The gathering of Alphas was intimidating to say the least. Each of these men and their mates were top of their particular food chain, and it showed. Each was dominant in a way that should have frightened Miranda, except for the fact that she had Mag at her side. He was easily the equal of any man in the room. His steadfast presence both physically and within her mind, reassured her in so many ways. His support allowed her to relax a bit and not react badly when a few of the more abrasive personalities challenged her.

There were a few moments before the meeting started where they mingled and Mag introduced her to a few new people. She got to say hello to the few she had already met, who were mostly members of Mag's family. After everyone was gathered, Grif signaled for the group to be seated in the great room of the house, which had been cleared a bit so that extra chairs could be brought in from the dining room and elsewhere.

Mag motioned her over to sit between Steve and his mate, Trisha, and Bob. Apparently there was a hierarchy even in the way these shifters sat around a room. Miranda wasn't too surprised by that. Vampires followed similar rituals and were probably even higher sticklers for formality. From what she could see, even though everyone had a prescribed place in the seating arrangements, they were mostly at ease, even casual in the way they spoke as the meeting started.

"All of you probably know by now that my brother Mag has been keeping company of late with Miranda van Allyn," Grif nodded toward her and she felt the scrutiny of every eye in the room fall upon her. Mag held her hand and gave it a little squeeze, which she appreciated. "They are old friends, and as you are all Alphas and leaders within the Clan, I think it's important for you to know that they are true mates."

Miranda tried not to gasp. She had never expected Mag's brother to broadcast the truth about their relationship to the Clan's leadership. Panic almost gripped her, but Mag's reassuring warmth in her mind helped her remain calm. He seemed to feel that nothing was amiss. She only hoped he was right.

A few of the gathered Alphas fidgeted at Grif's pronouncement as she looked around the room. She met one or two hostile gazes, but most were curious and a couple were downright shocked.

"For several reasons, the vampire Master has asked us to keep the true extent of their relationship under wraps. There are cultural taboos to such unions, as you all know. We've devised a plan that I think has merit. Miranda is going to be the new liaison between the Las Vegas vampire community and our Clan, and my brother Mag is going to be our liaison to the bloodletters. Now, we've never had liaisons before, but both Tony and I feel that this could benefit us all. The Master has pledged aid to us upon request and I've done the same."

"Help bloodsuckers?" That came from a woman near the edges of the room. She'd been introduced to Miranda as Shelley, mate of the badger Alpha. Apparently there was a small group of badger shifters working Redstone Construction, mostly on earthworks.

"There is precedent," Grif replied. "I talked to the Lords about all this at length and have their full approval. There have been all kinds of signs lately, but I'll defer to Kate for that part of this discussion." Grif nodded to the priestess who sat at his side. Both Kate and Slade sat opposite the Redstone family, on Grif's left. From the placement, Miranda knew the priestess and her mate held high rank in the Clan.

"Recently, there has been at least one other vampire-shifter mating that we know of. It was a *true* mating," Kate emphasized. "We believe the Lady Goddess may be preparing us all for a dark time to come. We all know the *Venifucus* has been hard at work, trying in many places, and in many ways, to restore Elspeth to this realm. If that happens, we'll all need powerful warriors to fight her." She paused, probably to let that concept sink in a bit.

"When a vampire drinks from a shifter, they gain shifter strength and magic, making them stronger than a vampire feeding solely on human blood," Kate went on to explain. "When a shifter mates with a vampire, he or she gains vampire speed and psychic abilities they don't normally possess. Together, they are stronger than either would be alone." Kate smiled, her entire manner easing this difficult conversation, and Miranda could see the priestess had the attention of every last person in the room.

"Only the pure of heart—those tested in ways that can seem cruel, but are ultimately strengthening—are chosen." Slade picked up the tale. "I'll be blunt. Miranda has been through hell. She was imprisoned by the madman who murdered the Redstone matriarch. Miranda was tortured, kept in a cage with silver bars, and repeatedly bled near to death, drained of magic and life. And yet, she survived." Slade paused to let his words sink in. Not many knew the full story of how Miranda had come to be with Mag.

"When I broke the magical circle in which she'd been held," Slade went on, "she attacked. I won't lie. She did some damage, and probably would have killed me. But all Mag had to do was call her name, and she came out of the blood frenzy that had gripped her. I've never seen an enraged vamp able to pull it together merely at the sound of her name. That she could do so after all she'd been through says something for her character. Miranda impressed me that night, as did

Mag. Their bond is true and strong. He is her anchor, as she is his. And together, they are stronger than either one of them is alone. In the future—if the worst happens and Elspeth is freed—we'll need their strength." Slade sat back and let that sink in.

"Mag suffered too," Kate said softly after a moment of silence. "He found his true mate more than two years ago, but because of the taboo, Miranda left him. Who among you wouldn't be insane by now if you'd found your true mate, only to have her leave without a trace?" Kate eyed every person in the room before continuing. "And none of us even knew it. Mag hid that soul-deep pain from us all for two *years*, and continued to be the dependable, hard-working man we all know and love."

Miranda could see the nods of approval and the fact that a lot of the listeners were impressed by what the couple had said. She would have preferred to keep her ordeal private— and she knew Mag felt the same—but if it helped their cause, she could live with it.

"I'm letting you all in on this information because you are the Alphas everyone looks to in the Clan for leadership." Grif took over the lead again. "I promised when you signed on with Redstone that there would be as much transparency as possible, whenever possible. I'm asking you to keep this information private for now. The Master and I both know that we won't be able to keep this secret forever, but we are buying as much time as we can for him to get his people in line. I'm not privy to all his plans, but I got the impression there's going to be a bit of house cleaning in the local bloodletter population soon."

That was news to Miranda. She'd assumed Tony would do something about Cassie sooner or later, but she didn't think beyond her sister. She should have. She knew the Master played deep games. It sounded like he was using this situation to do more than merely rein in her sister. Miranda hoped it wouldn't get too violent before it was all over, but when vampires went at it, blood was *always* spilled.

She almost dreaded what she feared was coming. Hanging out with the shifters, safe with her mate was probably the coward's way out, but if she was able, she would be doing exactly that until things settled down again.

"Because of that," Grif went on, "I'm advising you to keep your people close to home for the next few weeks. Especially the youngsters. The last thing we want is for stray shifters to get caught up in what should be a wholly vampire operation. I've agreed to aid the Master if asked. If we are called in, only a select few of our soldiers will be sent. I don't want innocents getting caught in the crossfire—and if news of Mag and Miranda's relationship gets out, the Master is well aware that any and all shifters could be hunted by unscrupulous bloodletters. Allowing them to dine on our blood indiscriminately is the last thing any of us wants."

Nods of agreement came from every corner of the room. That, at least, was something all the shifters could agree on. Miranda was glad to see the expressions of the few hostile shifters had changed over the course of the conversation. If they weren't exactly welcoming, they were at least thoughtful, which was a good start.

"I also expect you to minimize any hostility toward Miranda from the people under you," Grif added. "I've given you all the facts because I hope you'll see the need to accept what the Goddess has done in bringing a tried and tested vampire into our midst. I also expect you to lead by example and quell any misunderstandings about Miranda and her presence among us before they can turn into problems."

Miranda saw why Grif was such a popular leader. He didn't order his people to blindly follow his edicts. Instead, he explained things and gave his subordinates solid reasons for his decisions, encouraging them to help him implement his ideas. Even the stubborn faces she'd seen earlier had softened and were listening intently, nodding here and there when he made a good point.

The meeting went on for a few more minutes with every Alpha being given the opportunity to ask questions and speak their minds. It was a lot more democratic than Miranda had thought a shifter leadership meeting would be. She wasn't sure why she'd imagined they'd all be growling and pissing on each other to prove who was more dominant, but that's not the way the Redstones ran their Clan. She realized that was very likely the real key to their success.

Griffon Redstone hadn't amassed one of the largest and most successful collections of shifters in the United States around him by dominating every other Alpha in the group. He was a charismatic leader, it was true, but he also allowed each of the Alphas that had brought their various groups to the Clan a role in the leadership, and continued dominion over their own people.

It made sense. Otherwise, how could he manage such a diverse and populous group? While it was true the Redstone family was big, there was no way all the brothers—even if you added in their extended family—could be everywhere, and in charge of everything. It was a much smarter use of personnel to utilize the expertise that came with each new Pack, Tribe or Clan that came under the Redstone banner. Very smart indeed.

The meeting ended a short while later and everyone moved toward the back of the house where there were sliding glass doors that led to the big backyard. A grill was already lit and some of the folks carried platters of meat from the kitchen with them as they went outdoors. The barbeque was in full swing only minutes later and tubs of ice with beer, soft drinks and other choices were already waiting for everyone to serve themselves.

Mag pulled Miranda aside to a patio table where an ice bucket had been set up to cool a waiting bottle of wine. It was a bottle of one of Maxwell's finest vintages and Miranda had to smile at the Alpha pair's thoughtfulness.

"Lindsey ordered a few cases of wine when she heard we were mated," Mag explained, speaking of Grif's mate, a magical human who had been transformed into a cougar shifter in an unprecedented act of magic and faith. Miranda had liked her when they'd met, and her opinion only rose at the kind gesture of ordering wine just for Miranda.

That set the tone for the rest of the evening. Mag and Miranda sat on the patio and people came and went, speaking with them and learning more about each other. Miranda met everyone and started to form friendships with a few of the more open-minded shifters. Joe Nightwing, in particular, sat with them for a while, eating a huge, rare steak while they talked in low tones about the possibilities for upheaval in the vampire community.

He knew a lot more than most about the bloodletter power structure and was on a first-name basis with a lot of the key players. They compared notes on some of those he didn't know as well and discussed strategies for who could and could not be trusted. They speculated a bit on who might remain in the hierarchy after the dust had settled, but Miranda was glad that he didn't seem to be pushing for information she could not, in good conscience, reveal. She still owed some loyalty to her people, just as Mag did to his.

Grif and Lindsey joined them, sitting around the large patio table and joining in the discussion as they ate. Shifters could certainly pack away a lot of food, but Miranda was content with her wine. Occasionally she still missed being able to enjoy certain flavors, but bitter experience had taught her to not even try to taste things. Since becoming a bloodletter, everything tasted bad except the few things she could ingest.

"While I have you here, Alpha, there's something I'd like to speak with you about." Miranda broached a subject she had been thinking about for many weeks now. Joe Nightwing was still with them, but she'd come to trust his level-headed judgment over the past minutes.

"What's that?" Grif asked, casual yet alert.

"When I was being held prisoner, the mage often ranted about his *Venifucus* comrades and their plans. I was pretty incoherent most of the time but I do remember bits and pieces. I've begun writing down some of the things I remember him saying. They don't make a lot of sense right now, but I thought maybe, once I have my notes in order, I could give them to you. I figured if anyone would be able to make heads or tails of his ramblings, it might be you—or maybe the Lords."

Everyone at the table stilled. She knew it was presumptuous of her to even obliquely ask Grif to contact the Lords on her behalf, but really, that wasn't quite what she was doing. She merely wanted someone to have the information—someone who was actively working to oppose the lunatics that were trying to bring the Destroyer of Worlds back to this realm.

At length, Grif spoke. "I would like to see your notes," he admitted. "But I have to ask. Why would you give them to us and not to your people?"

"That's easy," she replied, feeling on firmer ground with his question. He wasn't suspicious of her information, merely of her reasoning in offering it to shifters and not vamps. "From all I've seen, you guys are actively working against the *Venifucus*. My people seem to be more caught up in their own little power struggles at the moment. I don't really know if the Master would care about my information. If it makes you feel better, I'll give him a copy too, but I don't have much confidence he'll be able to do much with it." She shrugged. "Mag told me that shifters have been gathering and sharing intelligence. I thought maybe my notes could help with that effort in some small way." She felt a little silly, but she really did want to give her notes to somebody, somewhere, who might be able to figure out what it all meant.

"Fair enough," Grif said after a moment's thought. "I'll be interested to see what you remember. You're right. We are sharing intel, and every little bit helps. Thank you for offering." He went back to his meal and the conversation flowed more easily from that point on.

When the shifters near the edges of the property began to disrobe and turn into animals, Miranda knew it was time to put on a little show of solidarity. Mag stood and stripped without a hint of self-consciousness. Of course, as gorgeously built as he was, he had no reason in the world to be self-conscious of his body. Miranda was glad though that she wouldn't have to get naked in front of everyone. Her magic allowed her to shapeshift without having to disrobe.

It was a different kind of magic than the shifters possessed, but at the moment all that really mattered was that she could become the female cougar and run alongside her mate. Miranda focused her magic and transformed, well aware that everyone around them was watching while trying not to stare. She felt their approval when she took her place at Mag's side and they loped off into the darkness together.

This was the first time she'd been able to run with him and their frolic took them around the perimeter of the Clan's lands, through a few backyards and into the desert a bit before they eventually found their way back to Grif and Lindsey's backyard. They chased each other, nipped and played, rolled around in the sand and batted each other with big paws that did no harm. It was a very freeing experience. One that she could not have imagined if she hadn't lived it.

She finally understood the appeal of becoming a four-legged beast once in a while and running her cares away. She'd have to do this more often with Mag. It would do them both good.

When they returned to the backyard, only a few of the guests had come back. Grif and Lindsey were still out roaming around, but Kate and Slade were sitting on a bench under a tree near a spot of lush greenery that was only a little out of place in the desert climate.

Kate called a greeting as they neared. "I wanted to tell you," Kate began as they drew closer, "I spoke with a close friend of Dante d'Angleterre's, and he's going to try to take some time to come out and meet you both. His name is Duncan and he's a very magical being according to the High Priestess. I'm not really sure what he is, but the Lords vouch for him. They were the ones who suggested I talk to him in the first place."

Miranda could feel Mag's surprise and acceptance through their link. The fact that the leaders of all the *were* in North America vouched for this guy carried a lot of weight.

"We'll look forward to meeting him," Mag answered politely.

"He might be able to shed some more light on your cross-species situation. He's well acquainted with the vampire-werewolf mating of his friends, Dante and Megan. The High Priestess hinted there was more to his story, but left it for him to reveal it or not."

"A man of mystery," Mag mused.

"Indeed," the priestess answered with a grin. She stood and her mate followed suit. "It was good seeing you again. Don't be a stranger, okay?" She reached up to give Mag a kiss on the cheek before sharing a brief hug and smile with Miranda. Slade merely nodded at them both as they took their leave.

Miranda was impressed that Kate seemed so at ease around her. There were few people who would dare come into her personal space once they knew what she was. The priestess was either brave or trusting. Maybe both. The more Miranda saw of her, the more she liked Kate. It was just possible, they could be friends. The thought intrigued her. Miranda hadn't had a real friend in decades.

Mag put his arm around her shoulders, squeezing her close to his side. No doubt he had picked up on her slightly melancholy thoughts. He was such a good man. Such a caring mate. Instantly her feelings brightened with the love she felt for him.

"Let's go home," she whispered, knowing he heard her.

"Your wish is my command," he replied, a slight growl in his voice.

They were thinking along the same lines. A frisson of heat coursed through her body as she picked up on his very naughty thoughts. Thoughts that mirrored her own. She couldn't wait to get home.

The first time they came together was hard and fast, and up against the wall in the garage. They were too hot to wait until they got in the house.

The second round was only a little less intense, and still in the garage. Mag laid her across the hood of his Lamborghini and admired the way she made the expensive Italian sports car look even better. He drove into her, reveling in the feel of his mate under him, willing to do whatever he wanted.

By the third time they joined, they'd finally made it inside the house. Mag had paused only long enough to secure the alarm system before depositing Miranda on the sheepskin rug in front of the fireplace in the living room. He lit a fire and before the embers had turned to flames, she had wrapped her arms around him. She unbuttoned his shirt from behind, tugging it off over his shoulders while he made sure the fire would be safe enough while they were...distracted.

Miranda took control this time, and Mag was more than happy to let her push him onto his back on the soft sheepskin. She worked her way down his body, undressing him as she went. When she had him naked, she did a little strip tease of her own, though her clothes were already in delicious disarray due to their earlier activities.

Both naked, she returned to him, straddling his legs to give him an enticing view of her body. She smiled, teasing her fingers over his skin, working their way up his thighs to the erection that stood hard and proud at the apex.

She didn't disappoint. Her soft hands felt marvelous on his most sensitive skin. She squeezed him, moving close and allowing her hair to brush the tops of his thighs as she lowered her head. The combination of sensations was subtle and exhilarating.

When her lips closed over him, Mag only spared a moment's thought for her fangs. They hadn't dropped, and he didn't expect them to. Not while she was going down on him. Miranda wasn't sadistic, and she was in his mind, in his heart. He trusted her. He also knew she could sense his thoughts—especially when they were making love.

Some guys might get off on the idea, but it wasn't something that appealed to Mag. He'd never been all that kinky, though his fellow shifters probably considered having sex with a vampire pretty kinky all by itself. The thought amused him, but a second later, all thought fled his mind as Miranda started to suck.

"Damn, baby," he whispered, throwing his head back on the soft sheepskin. "That feels so good."

She hummed in agreement and he felt the vibrations against his cock, increasing his pleasure. She was blowing his mind…among other things. But he didn't want to come without her. Watching and feeling her come increased both of their pleasure. The connection between their minds meant that the pleasure they felt mirrored back and forth between them, increasing the total effect for both of them.

He lifted her by the shoulders, easily handling her slight weight. Mag had always been strong—shifter strong—but now he had increased abilities due to his new mate. He knew she gained from being with him too, so he didn't feel any guilt about it. Hell, it came in handy at times like this. He was able to position the very willing Miranda to his exact desires. Over him. Ready to receive him.

He'd leave the joining up to her, letting her decide when and how to take him. Fast or slow, it was up to her. But he'd made it clear without words that he wouldn't be coming alone this time. Not ever again, if he had anything to say about it.

"So that's the way you want it, huh?" Miranda smiled at down at him, her hands on his chest. "I suppose your wish is my command, lover."

She sank onto his cock, taking him by storm. Fast and tempestuous seemed to be the order of the day as she began to ride him. He helped, guiding her hips and lending a little bit of his strength to help her keep up the pace she'd set.

It was fast and hard, mind blowing and fantastic in every way as she began to shudder over him. He came with her as her pleasure echoed through their connection, triggering his.

He followed her into rapture that went on and one between them, their minds, hearts and souls connected on a primal level that elevated them both to the stars and beyond.

They lay together in bed sometime later, both bare and breathing hard after an orgasm that had only come a little slower than all those that had preceded it. A trail of clothing led from the living room to the bedroom. Miranda had tried to gather up the bits they had discarded in front of the fire, but Mag had distracted her with kisses and she'd managed to drop most of them on the way to the bedroom. She smiled as she thought about how it must look.

Never in her life had she been so hot for a man.

"And you never will be again, love. Only me," her mate purred at her side, his hand idly stroking her skin.

Something occurred to her. "You heard me?"

Mag leaned up on one elbow, looking sexier than any man in history, she was sure. His golden eyes gazed down at her with a sexy, satisfied, almost feral light of both cougar and man. He was amazing.

"Glad you think so." He leaned down to kiss her, long and slow. When he broke the kiss and leaned back upward, her whole body was humming. "And yes, I do believe we've had a breakthrough. I heard your thoughts clear as a bell. In sentences, not just emotions or stray words."

She smiled and reached up to stroke his stubbly cheek, then tackled him so that she was on top. He laughed. Her big, predatory cat liked to wrestle and seemed to get off on the fact that she was as strong as he was.

"You're getting quicker too, have you noticed? Just a fraction, because bloodletters are already faster than just about any creature, but you're gaining the sure-footedness of my cat, which makes you even faster. Have I told you how much I'm enjoying the effect my blood has on you, baby?" He stroked his fingers over her hips and lower, to squeeze her ass. She loved the way he handled her body, his movements so sure, so perfect.

And now he could hear her thoughts. She wondered if she could hear his too.

"Can you hear me now?" he quipped, like the old cell phone commercial. He hadn't said it out loud, but she'd heard it. She giggled and her heart felt a kind of joy that only this man— her One—could bring.

"I love you so much, Mag." She lowered herself onto his body so that he was not only inside her, but so that she draped over him, her curves fitting so perfectly to his hard planes. The wetness of her tears mixed into the kisses she placed all over his face and throat. *"You are my life. My everything. My One."*

"You are the same to me, sweetheart. My mate. There will never be another you."

Their lovemaking was slow this time and so incredibly sweet. She rocked on him until they were both nearly incandescent with passion. Then he took over, rolling them so that he could bring her to the highest point of pleasure and hold her there, on the precipice, before finally allowing them both to tumble over together.

They lay together after, replete in each other's arms, basking in the closeness and the love. Dawn was approaching and she would sleep for the day while her lover did daytime things that they could never share. She felt sorry for herself for just a moment, but then thanked the Mother of All for giving her such a man. He could share her nights and still live in the sun. Miranda would never take that from him. She was glad he could still live a normal life in the daytime world, even if she could never join him under the sun's rays.

She went to sleep with that thought, and a prayer of thanks to the Mother Goddess uppermost in her mind.

CHAPTER TWELVE

When the call for help came in, it was unexpected. Mag and Miranda were both tapped as liaisons for the first time within hours of each other. Mag got the heads-up in the afternoon and sure enough, when Miranda woke after sunset, there was a message waiting for her as well.

Mag had gotten her a new cell phone and laptop weeks ago so she could get back into the swing of things with her business interests. She'd called her lawyer and accountant the night after they'd gone to the wine bar, and made them aware of her return to the States—or such was the excuse she'd used for her long absence.

She was pleased to learn that they had taken very good care of her finances while she'd been *away,* and were just as glad to have her back at the helm to give them further direction. She had spent a few hours here and there over the past weeks reestablishing her online presence, with Mag's help, and after their meeting with the Master, she'd been given special numbers and email accounts by which to reach him. The Master left her a message when her very first official job as liaison presented itself.

Mag greeted her with a kiss at sunset that evening. He also brought her up to speed on a situation involving his next oldest brother, Steve.

"Some wild stuff has been happening with Steve and his lady," Mag told her as they began their evening. "She was targeted by someone—a human, they think—who apparently killed that vampire downtown a while back."

It wasn't often an immortal was staked so publicly. The few times it had happened in the past, the entire vampire community in Las Vegas had felt ripples of unrest that lasted for weeks, until the perpetrator was caught. This time was no different.

The Master had contacted Grif directly when the murder had been discovered. Only after they'd discussed the problem leader to leader, had she and Mag been called. Should anything further develop, as liaisons, they were going to be on the front lines of it.

Mag had met the woman in his brother's life briefly. Steve had called him early one morning, desperate for a little familial support when the gal's father and brother showed up at Steve's house out of the blue. After meeting them, Mag could see why even his fearless brother Steve had called for backup.

It turned out that Trisha was not only the sister of one of Steve's human Army buddies, but she was also his mate. That little fact changed everything. She had apparently been raised to blend in with humans, but had an incredibly magical dad. Steve's Army friend turned out to be a non-magical half-brother, but he was very protective of his little sis. For that matter, so was their dad—an active duty, Navy Special Forces admiral.

Mag had met up with Grif and Slade before going to Steve's house. Slade had greeted the admiral and his step-son as old friends. Grif also knew them both from his days in Spec Ops. He'd introduced Mag and when the admiral got a good look at him, he'd felt the full weight of the man's scrutiny.

"This is Mag," Grif had said. "He's been liaising with the bloodletters for us."

"And letting them nibble a bit too, it appears," the admiral had quipped with a hard glint in his eye. The handshake the older man had delivered had been brutal, but Mag had learned to deal with big bad Alphas early on. His family was full of them. He wouldn't be cowed by this man, even if the admiral was reputed to make Navy SEALs cry like little girls on a regular basis. The admiral stared at the bite marks on Mag's neck and asked a whole lot with a single word. All he said was, "Voluntarily?"

Mag nodded under the older man's stare. "She's an old friend," he'd replied, adding a bit of Miranda's story.

"Just be careful not to give her too much," the older man had cautioned. "Vampires are unpredictable creatures at the best of times."

Mag didn't want to contradict the man, so he let it go. He knew Miranda's heart. She was his mate and he was her One. What the admiral didn't know…well…it didn't really matter. Mag's relationship with Miranda was private. And just about perfect, as far as he was concerned.

Mag had listened to the discussion and reported his information on the unrest in the vampire community when asked. When the admiral heard that the Las Vegas vampires were searching for a man who'd staked one of their own by night, plans began to form. Then Slade had revealed his intel. They knew the perpetrator's name, and that he was a low-level magic user. It seemed the *Venifucus* was involved to some extent, which Mag reported back to Miranda that night.

Miranda turned around and gave the information to Tony, fulfilling her role as liaison and then the discussions had been turned over to Grif and Tony, as leaders of their respective peoples. The liaison thing was working. They'd managed to get the right information to the right people in good time, and Grif had commented to Mag that he thought the new role suited him. Mag was glad to help. He liked that he was able to work with Miranda on Clan issues. It seemed a good use of their time and skills.

And so, when the planning started in earnest, they were as

ready as they could be to lend a hand. A major operation was being planned for downtown. Steve and his new mate, Trisha, were hoping to flush out the magic user who had been targeting her. It was believed the same man had also killed the vampire.

As a result, both the Redstone Clan and the Master vampire had agreed to work together. Miranda spent hours on the phone, coordinating the immortals Tony had asked to help. It was a little like herding cats, she'd joked, but she managed to pull them together and get them all to the Las Vegas strip at about the same time.

Mag was doing the same for the shifters, helping his brother Steve coordinate his security team with Miranda's people. The beginnings of a plan were set in motion and the only thing left was the execution. Mag would have looked forward to the action if the circumstances weren't so dire—and if Miranda weren't in the thick of it.

But as newly appointed liaison, she needed to be involved. Her people needed to see her doing her duty. Mag vowed he'd be at her side at all times. The two liaisons wouldn't go anywhere separately.

To that end, Mag and Miranda were pre-positioned in a hotel suite from which the evening's operation would be launched. Miranda was working the phones, setting up the coverage areas for the bloodletters while Mag kept the shifters updated on what the vamps were doing.

"Tony's people are ready," he told the gathering in the next room. Steve, Trisha, her dad and brother were all waiting for the signal to move. Once the vampires were in place, they could go at any time.

The bloodletters had been asked to use their psychic abilities to steer traffic away from Trisha as she walked down the Las Vegas strip. It was pretty well known that they could alter perception and influence what people saw—or didn't see. The idea was to draw the bad guy out into the open using Trisha as the lure. Then they'd move in and capture him, all while using the vampire's psychic gifts to keep regular humans unaware of the magical battle that took place right on the street.

Mag had thought it was a pretty tall order when the admiral had first suggested that part of the plan, but Miranda had merely nodded. She knew what her people were capable of and apparently, so did the admiral. Tony had agreed to the request and set Miranda on the task of organizing everything. Even Mag had been impressed by her ability to manage so many moving parts.

Miranda and Mag had to play their roles and stroll down the strip so her people could see her—see them both—as liaison. Mag kept a close watch over her, and he knew she was doing her part to steer regular folks away from the action on the sidewalk. They were about a hundred yards from Trisha, on the other side of the wide boulevard. Steve was out of sight, further up the road, but he'd be close if and when the trap was sprung. For now, Miranda was out in the open, aiding in the psychic deception.

Mag learned a lot that night. He saw how the bloodletters were able to target exactly who could see reality, versus the rest of the world that saw the illusion they created. He also learned about the different flavors of magic, and how vampires worked on a whole different level than most human magic users or most shifters, for that matter.

When the action really started, Miranda couldn't see much. She was busy actively steering humans out of the way and clouding their minds. But she did notice when two heavily armed men seemed to surf a giant wave out of the man-made lake behind Trisha. Whatever kind of magic those guys possessed, it was something she'd never seen before.

Then Trisha dove into the lake and did the same surfing thing on the way out. She had to be related to those military guys—or at least part of the same magical race. Miranda watched, working her own kind of magic on the humans all around, making sure her fellow bloodletters were doing the same.

When it looked like things had been resolved, Tony appeared. He greeted Miranda with a smile and a kiss on the cheek, like an old friend.

"You've done good work here, Miranda. I'm very impressed with your organizational skills." That he took the time to compliment her in the midst of so much tumult touched her greatly.

"I was glad to help," she murmured.

"I think it may be time to cross the street and offer our assistance," the Master said, his gaze straying to where Steve and Trisha stood on the pavement across the wide road.

Miranda kept up her psychic work while they crossed through traffic and made their way to the couple. Mag stood behind her, nodding at his brother's greeting but didn't make introductions, so Miranda took it upon herself.

"I'm Miranda," she said, reaching out to Trisha. "Your power is impressive." Miranda smiled, hoping to put the other woman at ease. After all, they were going to be sister-in-laws, of a sort, if Mag was to be believed.

"Indeed," Tony added, chiming in. "I suggest we move off the street. My people have strong influence over mortals, but we cannot be sure there are not Others watching our every move."

That seemed to sober everyone up and they walked as a group back toward the hotel from where they had started earlier that evening. They were silent until they'd reached the safety of the suite of rooms they had used earlier. There was already a bit of a crowd gathered there but Trisha and Steve stayed with Mag and Miranda for a moment while Miranda introduced them to the Master.

He was formal at first, but after a few moments of conversation, he seemed to mellow and invited them all to call him Tony. That was a bit of a surprise. The Master didn't often invite such familiarity. It meant he respected them and felt they were if not exactly *equals*, then at least powerful enough to have earned the right to use his given name.

When the two military guys from the lake arrived with an

older man, Trisha moved away to greet them with big hugs. They were, no doubt, her family. Miranda could see the resemblance now that they were standing closer.

"Those are some very powerful beings," Tony observed quietly, still standing next to Miranda.

"What are they? I've never seen anything like what they did back there," Miranda admitted.

"Water elementals of some kind," Tony said, watching the three men closely as he spoke. "Very magical in a way that we can never be. Such creatures usually don't become so heavily involved in mortal matters. It's strange to see them so ingrained in the human military."

"Really?" Miranda wanted to know more and the Master seemed in a talkative mood.

"If they show themselves in the mortal world at all, it is usually as environmental champions. Their power is tied closely to the elements and they have a vested interest in protecting the Earth."

Miranda saw the sense in that. She would have asked more, but the room was full and the after-action meeting was starting to take shape. Miranda listened with interest as they talked over the events of the night. Grif started by thanking everyone—especially the Master—then asked Tony to start the discussion by telling them all how much damage control they would need to do among humans who might've seen something.

"Certainly," Tony replied with his typical, engaging smile. "The elders of my forces were engaged in active illusion while the younger and less adept with such things were set to watch. We had only three instances where otherwise normal humans noticed some of the action. Each was intercepted and evaluated. Two were bespelled into forgetfulness. The other is still with one of my operatives. It is a woman. Her mind is resistant." The Master frowned as he reported that last bit. "I will go have a look at her as soon as we're done here and see what I might be able to do to mitigate the problem. Maybe one of your people would like to accompany me? The snowcat or his mate, perhaps?"

Kate and Slade agreed readily, so the Master went on. "Other than the three humans, only agents of the enemy saw what happened. All of those are accounted for—either dead or awaiting our questioning. They have been taken to a remote location and will remain under guard there until we are ready to talk to them."

It became clear that Slade and Kate would be in on the interrogation of the prisoners as well, and the meeting went on from there. Miranda leaned against Mag, her energy fading a bit. Even though she was feeling much better each day, when she used her powers for an extended period of time, she tired more easily than she should. It would take more time to build up her psychic muscles again to where they'd been before she was taken. Her skills were there, it was just the stamina that was lacking.

When the meeting broke up a short while later, Miranda was glad. The evening had been an adventure. It had ended well, and nobody was really hurt on their side. They'd even struck a blow for the good guys. All in all, it was a satisfactory result, but she was still exhausted.

Tony made a point of complimenting her work once more before taking his leave. He left via the balcony, alongside some surprised raptor shapeshifters. Apparently they'd never seen a vampire turn to mist before. Tony was old and powerful enough to have perfected the trick, and apparently wasn't afraid to show off a bit in front of the shifters.

Miranda and Mag left the old fashioned way—through the door and down the elevator to his waiting car. He drove them home while she relaxed. Before she knew it, they were back at the house in the desert and the night was half over.

Mag was a romantic at heart and he proved it yet again by carrying her into the house. He didn't stop until they were in the bedroom. He settled her gently on the bed, then left the room to make sure everything was locked up for the day. When he returned, expecting to find Miranda asleep once more, he was surprised instead by a naked sex kitten purring on his bed.

Apparently Miranda wanted to play a bit before she went to sleep. Mag didn't mind at all. He grinned as he stripped off his clothes, liking the way her gaze followed his every move. He drew out the process, doing a little strip tease of his own for her benefit.

"I hope you're enjoying this." He sent the words to her through their link, experimenting. Talking mind to mind was still so new to him.

"Mm. You know what I like," she sent back, the purr in her voice communicating through their minds. His little she-cat was turned on all right, and he wasn't far behind.

"This?" He asked as he stroked his hands over his torso, working downward. He pushed off his pants and boxers, then grasped his cock which was already hard and ready for action. *"Or this?"*

"All of it. Especially that," she teased with her words, her gaze zeroing in on his erection. *"I guess you're really happy to see me, eh?"*

"I'm always happy when you're naked in my bed, Miranda. You should have figured that out by now." He stepped out of the pile of his clothing and leapt onto the bed.

It was a simple jump for a man who shared his soul with a cat, but it seemed to take Miranda by surprise. She laughed and he loved the sound of her joy. He'd been so afraid for so long that she wouldn't be able to recapture the part of her soul that experienced happiness. Her ordeal had marked her in subtle ways, sure. It had changed her on a fundamental level, tempering her like a fine blade, making her stronger, but it hadn't taken away her ability to have fun. That pleased him more than he could say. Big cats liked having fun—especially with their mates.

He loomed over her, enjoying her petite form under him. She was so ladylike. So delicate looking. Yet, he knew, she had physical strength that nearly matched his own. Vampires were fast too. Even faster than shifters in some ways. She was his match in every way. Magical, strong, fast and yet soft, feminine and so very welcoming.

She opened her legs, making room for him between them. They didn't have to speak, not even in their minds. They were both clearly thinking the same thing. They both wanted to be as close as to people could physically be. Mag took his time, enjoying the moment of joining, knowing from the flavor of her thoughts that she loved it every bit as much as he did.

They came together and all was right with the world for one very long moment out of time. It couldn't last forever. Nothing ever did. But for this one moment, everything was as perfect as it could possibly be.

Mag would remember this moment—and many others just like it—whenever problems presented themselves. Which was far too often, as far as he was concerned.

CHAPTER THIRTEEN

The instant Miranda opened her eyes one night a few weeks later, she knew something was desperately wrong.

"Mag?"

"Here, love." He walked into the room from the adjoining bath, clearly having just stepped out of the shower. He had a towel wrapped around his lean hips and looked as edible as always, but she couldn't stop to admire him now. Something was seriously wrong.

She sat up, her gaze sliding over every object in the room as she sought the feeling of wrongness, and tried to figure out where it was coming from. Mag went on alert, the sexy grin sliding from his face to be replaced with a look of concern as he positioned himself between her and the door. He grabbed the tablet from the bedside table and quickly checked through the security screens.

"Nothing showing here. What do you sense?" he whispered.

"I'm not sure…"

Her cell phone rang loudly in the stillness. Miranda jumped. She couldn't help it. Her nerves were on edge, anticipating bad news. Mag reached for the small phone, glancing at the face of it before handing it to her.

"Blocked number," he said quietly, his brows drawing

downward in concern.

"This can't be good." Miranda handled the phone as if it were a live grenade, knowing already that she wasn't going to like hearing whatever would be said in the next few moments.

Mag grabbed his own phone and hit speed dial. She heard him talking in low tones with his brother Steve, the security expert, while her phone rang again. Then Mag addressed her.

"Answer it. Try to keep them talking as long as you can. Steve will run a trace."

Miranda would be impressed later, when she had time to breathe. Right now, she had to deal with whatever was waiting at the other end of the line. Sucking in a deep breath, she hit the button that would connect the call.

"Hello?" She did her best to sound as normal as possible.

"Miranda van Allyn?"

She didn't recognize the voice, and it had a slightly digital quality to it. Whoever it was, they were using some pretty high-tech equipment to try to disguise their voice, which said either it was someone Miranda *should* recognize, or someone obsessed with anonymity.

"Yes, I'm Miranda. Who is this?" She figured it wouldn't hurt to ask, and might add a few seconds to the call.

"That's not important," the caller replied. "What is important is that I have something you might be interested in."

"And what might that be? I can't think of anything I really need at the moment." She tried to sound bored, as if she had the upper hand, but deep down, she knew she didn't.

"It's not so much a *what* as a *who*. We know about the wine bar and the songbird. She's here now, as a matter of fact. Sadly, she's not very happy about being here."

Miranda began to shake—with fear or fury, she wasn't sure. "Let me get this straight." She stalled for time hoping to the Goddess that Steve was able to trace this call. "You've kidnapped one of my business partners? What do you hope to gain from such an action?" She didn't dare betray her true concern. The caller didn't appear to realize that Miranda was related to Mel. Miranda hoped to keep it that way.

"Go to the bar. Bring your phone. We'll call with further instructions. If you bring your pet, we'll know, and we won't call. In that case, the girl will die. It won't be pretty. Do you understand?"

"If this is about money—"

"Do you understand?" The voice cut her off angrily.

"I get it. Go to the bar and bring my phone."

"And no shifters. Not a single one, Miranda. You bring an animal with you, all bets are off and your friend dies in a really bad way. Got it?"

"Yes, I understand, but I need proof of life before I go anywhere. I want to talk to her."

"Good girl," the thought came clear as a bell into her mind from Mag. Their bond was strengthening.

There was a fumbling noise on the other end of the line and then a shaky, female voice came through the speaker.

"Hello?"

Miranda breathed a sigh of relief. It was Melissa. Thank the Mother of All.

"Mel? Is that you?" Miranda played for time.

"Yes, it's me. Randi? What's going on? Who are these people?" Her voice rose with her anxiety and Miranda cringed. They had to get her out of there. Wherever *there* was.

"It's all right. Sit tight, kiddo. I'm going to negotiate your release. Just be careful and stay alive for me, okay?" She wished she could say more but Melissa was utterly ignorant about the paranormal beings that surrounded her.

"Alive?" Mel's fear ratcheted up another notch. Damn. Miranda hadn't meant to scare her, but she needed to know the stakes here were very high. The highest, in fact—life or death. "Okay." Amazingly, Melissa calmed a bit, all on her own. That'a girl. "I'll do my best. Randi, I—"

Whatever she would have said was cut off as the first voice came back on the line.

"We'll give you one hour to get to the bar. Once you're in place, we'll call back."

The line went dead with a resounding click and Miranda smiled. She turned to look at Mag. He was still hanging on the open line of his phone, waiting to hear what Steve had to say.

"What?" he asked quietly, obviously noting her odd expression.

"He forgot to disguise his voice again on that last bit. I know who it was. A low-level vampire thug who works for Raintree. His name is Boris. You saw him the night we went to Raintree's club. Remember the goon who blocked our way up the stairs?" She stood and started getting dressed even as she thought more about their options. "Boris hasn't had an original thought in decades. That explains why he was talking in the royal *we*. He's operating on orders. Probably from Raintree."

Mag held his phone closer to his ear as she heard his brother speaking on the other end. It was a short message but it said so much.

"That clinches it. Steven managed to trace the call to the vicinity of Raintree's club." He ended the conversation with his brother with a promise to call back shortly.

"They're holding her there. Probably in that labyrinth of back rooms." She was certain of it.

"But they want you to go to Mel's bar," he pointed out. "Why?"

"To get me out in the open? I haven't been the easiest prey to corner lately. I'm always with you and we've been spending most of our time here. Even when we go out, we have a small army of shifters guarding us. If I go to the bar without all that, I'm easier prey."

"Then you stay here while we hit Raintree's and free Melissa." Mag was already getting dressed in a pair of black military-style pants with lots of pockets.

She'd never seen them before, but he looked comfortable in them and they didn't make a sound, indicating they were well-worn and had been washed many times to get rid of the fabric's natural stiffness. Her man was a badass commando and she couldn't love him more. But she also couldn't send him out into danger and sit idly by, waiting for word. She was going to be part of this.

"Rescuing Mel and leaving the real threat at the bar undiscovered isn't going to work. We free her and they'll just take her again. Or they'll do something else to someone else to flush me into the open. I think we need to nip this in the bud before anybody else gets caught up in it, hurt or even killed. I'm going to the bar."

Mag stilled, his gaze catching hers. "You can't go alone."

"I didn't say anything about going alone." She smiled, but it was a nervous smile. She was about to call on someone she wasn't a hundred percent certain was on their side. "Lend me your phone? Just in case they can somehow tap mine. Raintree shouldn't have had this number." She lowered her phone to the night table and held her other hand out for Mag's cell.

He seemed suspicious as he handed over the phone and she dialed in the number. It was answered on the second ring.

"Hi, Master Antoine?" It wouldn't do to call him the more familiar *Tony* when she was asking for help she wasn't sure he'd give. Miranda was well aware of Mag's surprise but he simply watched and listened as she outlined the problem to the Master and asked for his help.

Mag wasn't thrilled with the plan but he understood Miranda's reasons for wanting to end this tonight, before anybody else was hurt by their enemies. He kissed her deeply before he let her drive off into the night in his most heavily fortified vehicle. He had to let her go alone, in case anyone was watching.

But he knew something the watchers didn't. The Master vampire had promised to take to the air in his mist form and follow her path. If anybody attempted to waylay her before she got to the bar, he would render assistance. He was their ace in the hole. Mag just prayed Tony was as good as his word.

Mag suited up and went out behind his house as stealthily as he could. He had a pathway through the dark desert that would lead him to the rendezvous point he and Steve had arranged. Steve picked him up in the chopper—the big one, that could seat a platoon of soldiers, though Redstone Construction ostensibly used it for aerial tours for groups of clients.

Steve and Grif were at the controls, both familiar with such machines from their time in Army Special Forces. The back of the chopper was filled with a small group of family and friends who all worked for Steve in some security capacity. There were lots of weapons, some of which had been loaded with special ammo that would be especially useful against vampires.

They flew to the city faster than Miranda could drive, but they'd scheduled it so they'd start their assault on the back rooms of Raintree's club only after Miranda had arrived at the bar. With any luck the bad guys would be too occupied in both places to coordinate their response.

Grif landed the big chopper on the roof of one of the tall buildings near Raintree's. It was one that Redstone Construction had worked on recently, so they had all the access codes. It was child's play to commandeer the express elevator that would lead them directly to the basement level. From there, the little group would make their way stealthily toward the back alley behind Raintree's.

And from there, all hell would break loose in T minus ten minutes.

Miranda tried her best to hide her nerves as she walked into the wine bar. She hadn't seen a trace of the Master, but she hoped that was just because he was especially good at stealth. It didn't bear thinking that he'd lied and wasn't going to help her.

She didn't *want* to be all on her own here, walking into a trap, but if that's the way it was going to be, then she'd put up one hell of a fight before the end. Either way, she was as prepared as she was going to get.

She opened the inner, etched glass door and scanned the room.

There were few people here tonight. Far fewer than there should be. And those that were seated at tables and around the bar were not the usual human clientele.

Miranda began to sweat. Every last person in here was a vampire. At least a dozen of them. And none of them were people she liked. In fact, they were all either friends of Cassie's or Raintree's. Miranda didn't move in those circles, for good reason. The bloodletters gathered here were all on the shady side of the Light. Inhuman bastards, one and all.

This was *so* not good.

And then Cassie sauntered out from behind the bar.

"Glad you could join us, sister." Cassie oozed confidence and her hatred was almost palpable.

"What did you do with the mortals who normally work here?" Miranda feared they were all dead—or wishing they were. The group of vampires gathered here had little respect for their prey.

"I gave them the night off." Cassie looked around the place and smiled. "I'm going to enjoy running this place when you're gone. It has a certain class. I can see why you kept this under wraps. A nice little hunting ground reserved especially for you. Clever, girl. I'd admire you if I didn't hate you so very much." Cassie stalked closer and her smile turned evil. "Tonight I will finally have my revenge and it already tastes so damn sweet."

Cassie reached for her, but Miranda sidestepped. She moved so fast that not even Cassie could match her. Damn. Mag was right. His cat's reflexes were honing her already preternatural speed into something even more formidable. She'd need all of it to get out of this confrontation alive.

Miranda was ducking and dodging with the best of them and admiring her own new skills when a steely grip caught her from behind. One of Cassie's friends had caught her, and his grip was strong. But was Miranda stronger?

She tried to break free, and though it was a bit of an effort, she discovered she was up to the challenge.

Next they started throwing things at her. Glasses and bottles escalated to chairs and tables, but she was able to dodge them all, speeding around the room. The bar was being trashed though. There would be a lot of work needed to bring the place back up to snuff after this was all said and done. Miranda only hoped she was still around to foot the bill.

Cassie screamed in rage as she and the other dozen bloodletters chased her around the bar. Miranda had the advantage in several ways. First, she was just a hair faster than the others. Second, she was stronger than every single one of them. Even if someone managed to get a hand on her, she was able to break free in seconds. Third, she knew the bar better than any of them. She'd been involved in the design and construction of the place from day one. Mel had overseen the day shift and Miranda had come to watch the night shift finish things. Theirs had been a very active partnership in the beginning.

Miranda had enjoyed getting to know her niece. She only hoped she'd be around to continue their acquaintance. But she was tiring. Her opponents knew she couldn't keep up this pace indefinitely. Things were going to change sooner or later.

And then they did.

The door opened and everyone in the room froze in place as a new person entered the building.

The Master had arrived.

Miranda could have wept. Tony was playing the part of the cavalry...or was he? She waited along with the rest of them, to see where he stood on the matter of Miranda's life—or death.

"My children, playing tag is not recommended indoors," Tony observed, pulling off one of his leather gloves a finger at a time. Everyone in the big room watched to see what he would do, perhaps none as eagerly as Miranda. "Cassie dear, would you please explain the meaning of all this?" He waved negligently around the room, one hand still holding his silver-tipped cane—a rather human affectation, Miranda had always thought.

"Sure," Cassie said defiantly, stepping toward the Master. "Why not?" She sneered at the man she had previously sworn to obey. My, how times had changed. "Since you decided to do *nothing* about Miranda and her pet, we took it upon ourselves to corner her and kill her. Once we're done with her, the cat will be next."

"You would start a war with the most powerful shifter Clan in the United States?" Tony observed, one eyebrow rising in the merest show of interest. "All because of one little vampire and her mate?" Tony made a tsking sound as he shook his head. "You disappoint me, Cassandra. You and all those who've gathered behind you. And Raintree. Don't think I don't know who's behind all of this."

"What of it? Soon you'll be dead and Raintree will wear the mantle of Master." Cassie was really pushing her luck, Miranda thought. It was one thing to threaten a relatively low-level being like Miranda. It was another thing entirely to defy the Master to his face.

"You think so?" Tony's voice had dropped to a low pitch that held a world of warning in it. Apparently Cassie couldn't or wouldn't hear it.

"I know so," Cassie replied, raising her chin in defiance.

Tony was a blur as he crossed the space between himself and Cassandra. The knob of his cane came out, and he threw the long stick aside revealing…not a sword…but a stake. A wooden stake that he pushed straight into Cassie's chest.

She clutched at his hands as she died, falling slowly to the floor as the Master stood over her. The look on his face was one of stern regret.

"I take no pleasure in ending a life, but defying me in my own domain cannot be tolerated." Tony looked up at the rest of the bloodletters who watched with varying expressions.

Most didn't seem to care that Cassie was done for. A few

seemed taken aback, but still defiant. It was clear to Miranda that the battle wasn't over. Not yet.

"Miranda, do you serve the Light?" The Master snapped his question out like a whip. It caught her by surprise, but the answer came out of her mouth without thought.

"Always," she replied.

"Then you may serve in my court." Tony nodded with an old world charm. Sort of like a liege lord bestowing a boon on his vassal. For all she knew, maybe he had been such a lord. He certainly knew how to act the part. "The rest of you," Tony addressed the dozen bloodletters that remained. "If you serve the Light and agree to abide by my rule, you will be spared. If you continue to side with the forces of evil, you will either leave or die. What say you?"

"The Light never did me one damn bit of good," one ruffian spoke up. He was a friend of Cassie's. Rough around the edges, he was a young vampire who had only been made recently. "The night I woke up a vampire, I gave up all things associated with the Light. And the day I killed my first man—I was only a teenager—I decided then and there that the devil could have me, 'cause God sure wouldn't."

"Think carefully on your words," Tony warned. "Vampire I may be, but I have served the Mother Goddess all my nights and will continue to be Her servant for all the nights I have left. I will not ally myself with those who oppose Her goodness. You will either leave my domain or die by my hand. Your choice." Tony eased back, his stance going loose. Ready for anything.

Miranda took her cues from him. He had lived centuries. He knew how to win a fight. She could do worse than learn from an expert like the Master. She dropped back into a ready stance. If they were going to attack, it would be soon.

Mag didn't dare break into Miranda's thoughts, but their connection was close enough now that he was aware of her situation. He'd known the moment she'd walked into the bar, and he'd given the signal to the team to start their operation at Raintree's. He was acting in a support capacity for now, keeping mental track of his mate through their connection without doing anything to distract her.

Mag knew when Tony waltzed into the bar, and felt Miranda's surprise when he staked Cassie without blinking an eye. Wow. Mag hadn't realized Tony had it in him. Not really. He'd known intellectually that the man had to have balls and superior fighting skills to claw his way to the title of Master. Mag had just never seen it in action.

He kept one part of his mind on the wine bar while the rest of him brought up the rear as the small team of shifters infiltrated through the back alley at Raintree's. It wouldn't take long before their presence was discovered, but he caught the scent of their prey almost the moment he stepped inside the back entrance of the club.

The guards—human guards—that had been stationed in the back of the club were knocked out and tied up. Not a sound had been made to betray the shifters' presence. Mag had to admire his brother's security team. They had serious skills.

None of the others had met Melissa, so Mag gave the signal to his elder brothers. He'd take point to locate the room where she was being held. It wasn't far. He knew that for a fact. His nose told him so.

Melissa shared the roses and cinnamon scent of her great aunt, but to a lesser degree, and it was tempered by her human side. That, and the wine that surrounded her working hours had left its traces in her scent. It was an easy scent trail to follow in the miasma of humans and vampires that populated the rest of the dance club.

One short hallway and three doors later, Mag located the room. He scented one vampire in there with her, as well as a human female. And fresh blood. Shit.

Mag nodded to Steve when he gave him the signal. Of the group, Mag was probably the fastest now. And Melissa knew him. She'd be less likely to freak out if she saw him enter the room and incapacitate the bloodsucker.

In Mag's mind, connected as he was to Miranda's thoughts and emotions, he felt the standoff happening at the wine bar. He shut that part down for a moment so he could concentrate on his task. He'd hit this hard and fast, and all would be well. Taking a deep breath, Mag kicked open the door, storming into the small room.

The vampire didn't know what hit him. One minute he was snacking on a half-naked human woman, the next, he was up against the wall with Mag's hand on his throat. The fangs didn't scare Mag, and when the bastard tried to shapeshift, Mag punched him in the throat, cutting off his air. A heavy tap on the head put the bastard down for the count.

Mag left the unconscious vamp to his brother's people. They had ways to secure him that he wouldn't be able to escape. He also left the bleeding woman to one of the female shifters on his brother's team. Mag went for Melissa.

He untied her and loosened the cloth gag that was tied around her face.

"We need to be quiet, but we're here to get you out. Are you okay to walk, Melissa?" he asked quietly as he worked.

"Magnus? What the hell? That guy is a vampire!" She was definitely freaking out, but managing to keep it down as well. So far, so good.

"Yes he is, Mel," Mag confirmed. "And there are more of them in the immediate vicinity. I'm here to get you out as quietly as possible, but if we have to fight them, we will, and it won't be pretty. Stand up, honey." He supported her as he lifted her to her feet but she was feisty and batted his hands away.

"I can do it," she insisted. "Where's Randi?"

"Fighting them at your bar," he answered honestly. "They lured her there but we figured out you were being held here so we split up."

"You let her go alone?" Mel was getting angry. Mag liked her spirit.

"Not exactly. She's got a seven hundred year old vampire fighting on her side. And once we get you to safety, I'm going to go help her, so let's get a move on, okay?"

"Yeah," she replied, walking unsteadily toward the broken door. "I got it. Let's go."

At the wine bar across town, the young vampire attacked first, and went down just as quickly while his fellows watched. That left eleven for Miranda and the Master to deal with.

Eleven against two. The odds still sucked.

Miranda knew Mag was busy, and she didn't dare distract him, but she felt the moment he found Mel. His emotions reached out to her, humming in the back of her mind. She knew he wasn't out of danger yet, but he'd found Mel and she was alive. Of that, at least, Miranda was certain.

Knowing that, she felt a moment of relief. It made what was about to come next somehow easier, knowing her grandniece was in good hands. She trusted Mag and his Clansmen to see to Mel. They would get her someplace safe.

"Do you know what a *Chevalier de la Lumiere* is?" the Master asked almost conversationally as he touched the bloody tip of the wooden spike he still held in his right hand.

That piece of wood had already killed two vampires. It would see a lot more action tonight if these assholes didn't back down.

"A Knight of the Light?" Miranda spoke her thoughts aloud. She'd heard whispers of such beings, but thought they were merely a legend.

"A fairytale," one of the older vampires scoffed.

"I thought so too," Tony agreed. "Until I met one." Disbelief showed on the faces of their enemies all around, but the Master definitely had their attention. "He gave me a means by which to summon him. If you persist, I may have to use it."

The younger bloodletters seemed uncomfortable but the older ones looked unimpressed, Miranda noticed. Not good. They were probably going to have to fight their way out of this after all.

"You'll be threatening us with hobgoblins next." The

older vamp, who seemed to be the new spokesman for the group sneered. "You're weak, Antoine. You always were. We should've challenged you long ago."

Tony laughed out loud, shocking Miranda a little. "None of you are strong enough to take me in a real Challenge—a fair fight. This is cowardly, but I should expect no less from people who align themselves with the *Venifucus*."

Miranda gasped but saw no argument on the faces of the eleven left facing them. They *were* in league with the *Venifucus*. She was appalled. Only truly twisted minds would ally themselves with a group that wanted to bring back the Destroyer of Worlds.

"You saved us some effort, Antoine," the spokesman went on, coming closer. "After we dealt with the animal lover and her pet, our next stop was your place."

"Since you cannot be dissuaded, I see no reason to delay." Tony took a ready stance as if to invite the attack.

A moment later all hell broke loose. Again.

The eleven who were left split up. Three of the younger ones went after Miranda and the rest centered on Tony. She wasn't dodging them this time. No, she'd learned from the earlier skirmish. This time, she was using her superior strength and going for the kill. She would have to hit them as hard and fast as she could before they overwhelmed her or Tony…or both.

She fought like a she-cat, clawing and scratching, using her abilities to shift into monster shapes that served her well. Her hands became razor-tipped claws that pierced deep into flesh. She took out one of the attackers right away by piercing his heart. Her claws weren't exactly wooden spikes, but they did a pretty good job all the same.

Tony took out one of his own, leaving nine total. They were doing well, but this was a losing battle. The two of them couldn't hold out long enough against such odds, even if they had superior fighting abilities. Something had to change the equation.

And then she felt magic gathering. Fierce golden, pure-toned magic coalescing out of the air. What was left of the drum kit on the small stage began to vibrate, as did the few crystal wine glasses that hadn't already been shattered. Something was happening, but she had no idea what it was— and most importantly, whether it was good or bad.

CHAPTER FOURTEEN

Mag had Melissa nearly to the door of Raintree's club when the man himself blocked their path.

"Leaving so soon?" Aramis Raintree oozed confidence with his smug grin. Mag growled, wanting nothing more than to rip out the bastard's throat. Miranda was in trouble. As her mate, Mag felt an urgency to finish this quickly so he could go to her.

He took a quick look around and formulated a plan. It would take all his newfound speed, the strength of his shifter blood, and all the dexterity of his cat to do it, but he had confidence in his own abilities. Raintree was dangerous. An old one. Second only to the Master.

If war broke out between this particular bloodsucker and the small group of shifters, it would be a bloodbath. A lot of people could be hurt before Raintree was subdued. *If* they could subdue him at all. And all the while, Miranda was in jeopardy.

Mag nodded to Grif and subtly handed Melissa off to the nearest shifter. To Raintree, it probably looked as if he was merely preparing room to fight, and he was. But he doubted Raintree—or anybody, really—expected what he had planned next.

In a blur of motion, Mag grabbed a mop that had been

leaning against the wall near him and broke the wooden shaft in two. Armed with two very pointy, wooden stakes, Mag sprang at the vampire before Raintree even seemed to realize what was happening. The bastard tried to move out of the way at the last moment, but Mag was just that much faster than Raintree.

He was pinned and staked in no time flat. One piece of the mop handle piercing his throat and driving all the way into the cinder block wall behind him, the other rammed right through his black heart.

Raintree was well and truly dead.

"Holy shit, bro," Bob broke the stunned silence as everyone remained motionless, just looking at what Mag had done.

It had taken less than a moment to down one of the strongest vamps in the city. Even Mag was impressed by his own speed. As he looked around with grim determination, the rest of the team seemed to wake up from their momentary shock. Steve assessed the situation.

"First priority, get the hostage to safety," Steve reminded everyone in a quiet, steady voice.

"Let's go," Grif added. The team began to move, having to pass Raintree's body on the way out the back door of the club. Leaving him there would serve as a warning to any of his sycophants who might try to pick up where he left off.

But Mag didn't think any of his close followers were at the club tonight. No, the real army of baddies was over at the bar, facing off with Miranda and Tony. They'd been overly confident and had split their forces unevenly. Raintree had remained in the relative safety of his club with only one of his vampire thugs guarding the hostage while he sent everyone else out with Cassie to take down one small woman.

As it turned out, he had been right to be scared of Miranda. She was more than they knew. She'd gained a lot from mating with Mag—as he'd gained from being her One.

Mag desperately wanted to tell her that he was on his way, but he didn't want to distract her. He kept a sort of peripheral awareness of what was happening at the bar through their connection, but they'd both agreed to keep the line of communication mostly closed so they wouldn't run the risk of distracting each other at a critical moment.

The shifter team's exit was uneventful. They went back the way they'd come and Mag jumped into the helicopter, impatient to go help his mate. He went toward the cockpit, needing to talk to his brothers.

"Miranda needs help," he said quietly. "Drop me at the bar on your way out of town."

Grif looked at him with new respect, and simply nodded as they lifted the chopper off the pad. A quick, slightly unauthorized flight path over the buildings of downtown took them within feet of the roof of the bar. Mag didn't wait. He merely looked for his opportunity, then jumped out of the helicopter onto the roof of a nearby building. He could make his way down from there.

He paused only a moment when a few others made the jump right after him. Bob was the first one, followed closely by Matt. When a giant owl swooped in under the rotors and landed on the roof, someone in the chopper threw out a knapsack that made a thunking sound as it landed on the roof. The owl shapeshifted into the form of Joe Nightwing. He threw a lazy salute up at the retreating helicopter as he retrieved the bag.

"I have the rest of my team patrolling the skies but I figured you could use some help," Joe said quietly, already throwing on the clothing from the pack.

There were weapons in there as well—a .45 caliber handgun and a utility belt that had sharp wooden stakes hanging off it. Joe strapped it on quickly as he moved along the roof behind the Redstone brothers.

Mag knew Steve and Grif would have been there too, but they were needed to fly the chopper, to get Melissa to safety. The female members of the team had stayed with Melissa in the back of the helicopter. They'd take her to Clan lands and help her calm down. She had looked pale and a little shell-shocked to Mag's eyes as he jumped out of the chopper, but he hadn't had time to coddle her.

She'd seen a lot tonight and she'd probably have to be let in on the reality she'd just discovered. She'd seen a vampire feeding, and another being staked. She'd seen guys jump out of hovering helicopters, and had probably watched Joe shift from owl to human. The cat was truly out of the bag as far as Melissa was concerned, but they'd deal with it later. Miranda would probably enjoy not having to hide herself from her niece—as long as Mel was able to accept her. That would be the big hurdle, but that was for later—if they all survived.

Now was for helping his mate and killing vampires. Mag suppressed a growl. He wanted them all dead. All those who dared threaten his mate were fair game as far as his cougar was concerned, and it was time to go hunting.

Nine evil vampires were doing their best to destroy what was left of the wine bar on their way to killing Miranda and the Master. Tony was holding his own against six of them while Miranda did her best to fend off the two who were concentrating their efforts on ending her immortal life.

She was facing none other than Boris—the bastard who had called with the news they had kidnapped her niece. Beside the thick-necked Boris was a tall, skinny vampire known for his speed. Gene was a bit of a nerd, but not in a lovable way. No, Gene had creepy down to a science. He reminded her of the type of guy that pulled the wings off bugs as a child, then escalated to torturing small animals, and eventually to serial killer status. Only Gene had been turned before he'd made his mark on the human world, and his maker had held him in check—or at least taught him how to hide the bodies so that mortals would never find them.

His maker, a psycho Miranda wanted no part of, was even now fighting Tony. She was a good friend of Cassie's named Gretchen. Rumor had it she'd been a supporter of Hitler and many tyrants before him, and possibly a camp follower with Hannibal's army. She was an old and powerful bloodletter who usually liked to manipulate events from the shadows. For her to have stepped forward in this particular action meant something. Something very sinister.

Boris and Gene had grown cagier after seeing the way Miranda had taken out their friend. They were even more wary of her now. They knew for certain that she wasn't as vulnerable as they had thought, and they were acting accordingly. One would feint while the other raced in to score a hit on her.

Miranda was bleeding from a half dozen cuts but then again, so were her enemies. There was a delicate balance...for now. She knew in time, she would tire and make a mistake. They would be all over her then. But she had to hold out just a little longer. She felt in her heart that Mag was on his way. She'd known when he had freed Melissa. She felt him draw closer, their bond reasserting itself with his proximity.

She sent a silent prayer to the Mother of All. *Please let him be in time. And please don't let him be hurt or killed in trying to help us.*

She felt a new magic tingle, as if in answer to her prayer. A golden-hued magnificence that started small and grew exponentially in the middle of the chaos that was the bar-cum-battlefield. Tony and the bulk of the bad guys were down on the dance floor and demolished seating area, while Miranda battled her two opponents a few steps up in the bar section near the door.

Their enemies didn't seem to notice the magic tingle at first. Not until a blinding golden-white light exploded in the center of the room, between the two battling groups.

In the center of the light was a man. No. Not a man. A knight. Dressed in armor of shining golden light.

And then he began to move. He took on half of Tony's opponents, taking the strain off the Master. Miranda didn't have time to really get a good look at the guy because she was busy fighting for her life, but everyone noticed when he started running vampires through with a golden sword that chimed each time it struck a blow.

The sound distracted her just enough. Boris grabbed her from behind, immobilizing her long enough for Gene to pounce...but he never got there.

The inner, etched glass door of the bar shattered as Mag roared, racing inside to stake Gene through the heart. The lanky vampire staggered and dropped, the wooden stake sticking out of his back as his lifeblood wept onto the floor.

Mag kept coming, ignoring the fallen. Their eyes met and Miranda felt Boris quake in fear behind her. It had finally occurred to him that this was not going to end well for his side. Miranda smiled at her One as she saw two of his brothers file in behind him. They paused only a moment before going to help Tony and his golden-knight friend. Mag waved them on with a gesture that radiated confidence.

"You should let her go now," Mag advised Boris in a low, growly voice.

"I let her go, you let me walk out the door." Boris's voice shook and Miranda half expected him to wet his pants. From up here, he could probably see the tide had turned, even if his fellows below on the dance floor were still caught up in the heat of battle.

"Sorry. Can't do that. But if you let her go, I might let you live. How's that for a bargain?"

Boris seemed to think about it for a moment longer and then he let go all at once, his hands in the air. Miranda turned on him and punched him hard across the face. Boris flipped around from the force of the blow and landed on the floor. He looked up at her, stunned.

"That's for kidnapping my business partner and wrecking our bar. I could've broken free of your hold anytime, Boris. Remember that. If you come after me or mine again, I will kill you and dance on your bones." She leaned over the cowering vampire menacingly.

Mag placed a hand on her shoulder, calming her rage a bit. She stepped away from Boris, who wisely stayed right where she'd dropped him. Another figure stepped forward out of the shadows. It was Joe, the owl shifter she'd met once before. He had heavy duty restraints in his hands that he used on Boris while Mag and Miranda shared a brief hug. Reassured that they were both really okay, they turned as one to wade into the fray that continued to center around Tony. The very magical knight fought back to back with the Master while Bob and Matt worked the periphery of the knot of combatants. Miranda caught sight of one particular enemy she wanted to coral.

"Gretchen is trying to weasel away," she told Mag. "We can't let her go. She'll go to ground and turn some more budding serial killers to be her children. It's sort of her thing."

Mag didn't comment but followed where Miranda led, toward one side of the big room where a blonde woman was doing her best to sneak away. While they worked their way over there, the knight took out another vampire with a chime from his sword. The Master got another a moment later. The two men seemed to be enjoying themselves now that the odds were getting better.

Mag peeled away from Miranda's side as she made her way down and to the floor area. She would confront Gretchen head on while Mag provided backup.

"Going somewhere?" Miranda challenged as Gretchen stopped short. Miranda blocked her path—her cowardly way out of the battle still in progress.

"Get out of my way, bitch. I don't care who you've been dining on. I'm older and stronger than you any day of the week." Gretchen wasn't what you'd call a good sport. She snapped like a viper when cornered, and she was snapping now—all bark and no bite.

"You want to test that theory?" Miranda detested the woman and it came through in her tone. "I'd love to put a stake through your heart. Just give me a reason."

"I don't have to answer to you. You're just a child. Survive for a few more centuries. Then look me up." Gretchen tried to bluff, but it wasn't going to fly.

"You'd better believe you're going to answer to me, bitch.

You think you're so smart, pulling everybody's strings from behind the scenes. Well, you miscalculated big time tonight, Gretchen." Miranda was shaking, she was so angry.

It suddenly became clear how much influence the conniving bitch had peddled to push this uprising. For it was obvious this wasn't just a plan to get rid of Miranda and Mag, but it was a maneuver to ultimately take out the Master himself. No doubt some puppet like Raintree wanted to take his place. A puppet that owed Gretchen for putting him in power.

A glance toward the center of the room told her all she had to do was stall Gretchen for a few more moments. The battle was almost over. Only two vampires left, caught between the Master, his glowing, well-armed friend, and two pretty fierce Redstone brothers. It was game over. All it needed was the grande finale.

It came a moment later when Tony and his friend took out the last two—one each. They looked around the room to see who was left, and Miranda knew the moment they spotted her, still blocking Gretchen's path. Gretchen knew it too. She made a frustrated growling sound and launched herself at Miranda.

But Miranda was ready. She easily held off the older vamp, and a moment later, Mag was pulling the woman off her from behind. Gretchen squirmed in his hold, but she couldn't break it. Mag turned the woman toward Tony, launching her through the air to land at the Master's feet in an ungraceful sprawl.

Tony looked down at the disheveled, blood-stained woman.

"I'm very disappointed, Gretchen. I thought you had changed your ways, but I see now that I was wrong." Tony shook his head, his clothing ripped and blood-stained, his hair hanging in messy clumps around his face. He had the light of battle still in his eyes.

"Gretel? Is that you?" the knight spoke for the first time, leaning down to peer at the Gretchen's face. "I thought you long dead, but I see now I was deceived. Of course, you're very good at deception. I know that first-hand."

All eyes turned to the knight. "You two know each other?" Tony asked.

"I knew her in the distant past. She was called Gretel then, when she fought on the side of Elspeth in the last great war. I suppose you serve her still?" the knight asked Gretchen directly.

"I will always serve the side of strength and power. The Destroyer knows how to deal with mortals and mongrels." She sneered at the shifters who had formed a semi-circle behind her.

The knight sighed heavily, resting on the hilt of his sword. "Judgment was passed against you millennia ago Gretel, for crimes against humans, shifters and immortals alike. Crimes against the Light. The Lady Herself witnessed your evil and laid down the penalty. I thought it carried out long ago, but I see that I must do it now. Prepare yourself."

Fear entered Gretchen's eyes. She looked around the room as if seeking some way out. If she made a break for it, Miranda would be ready. It sounded like Gretchen had done a lot more than Miranda knew about, but the knight seemed to have her number…and her punishment.

Light began to emanate from the knight. Brilliant, golden-white light that caused the room to vibrate and the sword to chime. Lovely, lilting notes that filled the air with their magic. For this was true magic—the highest form of it. The magic of other realms brought to earth. Something Miranda had heard about in fairytales, but had never thought she'd ever see in person.

"Do you repent of your evil ways?" the knight asked in a booming voice as the light grew in intensity. Gretchen cowered in fear, a kind of paralysis seeming to have taken her ability to move.

"I hate you! I hate you all!" Gretchen cried out in defiance. "Elspeth will get you and then I will be reborn. She will bring me back as my comrades will bring her back…" Her words trailed off as the light nearly blinded everyone in the room.

Miranda blinked, but watched as best she could. She saw Gretchen…dematerialize…if that was the right word. As the light engulfed her, she became particles of darkness within it, bathed in the golden glow until they dissipated into the ether. Until finally, Gretchen was gone. Completely just…gone.

And then the light pulled back, dimming and retreating to wherever it had come from. The knight had a hard expression on his face, but he seemed at peace with what he had done.

"Wow." Bob uttered, closer than Miranda to the strange knight. "All the bodies," he pointed out. "They're gone too."

"As is Boris," Joe reported from the bar, holding up the empty, still-locked restraints. "Just like the woman. Dissipated by the light."

"And your cuts are healed," Mag said from beside her, stroking her arm with his hand. She looked down and realized that all the damage she'd sustained in the fight was gone. Healed by the light.

She looked around, taking stock of everyone, starting with Mag. "We're all healed," she marveled. She knew who had caused this phenomenon. She turned back to the man in the glowing armor and bowed her head slightly. Respectfully. "Thank you, sir knight."

"You don't need to thank me. It was the Lady's will. She whom I serve determined the course her power would take. It was She who answered your prayer and allowed me to appear here and do Her bidding." He bowed slightly and Miranda realized something.

"You're the *Chevalier de la Lumiere* the Master was talking about."

"Guilty as charged. And you are the youngster who has found her One in an unlikely place. From the way he looks at you, and the energy around your spirits, I take it this is your mate?" The knight inclined his head toward Mag.

Mag nodded. "Magnus Redstone. And these are my brothers, Bob and Matt. And the Alpha of our Clan's fliers, Joseph Nightwing." He introduced all the shifters in the room.

"And I'm Duncan le Fey. I've been meaning to get in touch with you two."

Tony turned to the knight and shook his hand. "Thank you for coming, Duncan."

"Anytime, brother." They shook hands and clapped each other on the back as they shared a manly, half-hug.

CHAPTER FIFTEEN

"Your timely arrival was much appreciated," Tony said formally to them all. Duncan stood quietly by his side once the dust settled.

"Looked like your friend there had things well in hand." Joe smiled as he spoke, his respect for Duncan's power clear in his dark eyes.

"Yes, but the fact that you came to my aid speaks well for your people, and our alliance." Mag knew Tony was a diplomat, but sometimes things needed to be stated unequivocally. Apparently this was one of those times. "Please carry my thanks to the Alpha. Tell Grif I'll be calling him as soon as I have my house in order. Things are going to change in the city, so it might be best to have your people keep clear for a little while, until things settle down."

All four shifters frowned. The fey knight noticed and joined the conversation.

"What my colleague is trying to say is that he's about to come down hard on the side of Light. Events have been building up to this declaration for a while, and it can no longer be avoided. Basically, he's going to give any immortal who refuses to declare themselves to the Light, their walking papers. They either leave his domain or suffer the consequences. We're making a stand here, gentlemen. It would be best if your people weren't put in the path of any unscrupulous immortals who are on their way out of town."

"You said that during the fight," Miranda said into the silence. "You told them they had to choose."

"And the dozen we fought chose the wrong side," Tony confirmed in a no-nonsense tone.

"The next logical step is to take the ultimatum to the wider audience. When he makes his stand, there are going to be a few unhappy vampires in this city. Warn your people," Duncan reiterated.

"We'll do that, but we can also be of help. This alliance is real now. We're in this together," Mag assured the knight and the Master both.

"In fact," Joe drew their attention, "if I may, I'll go along with you two tonight. I'll provide air cover, if you like. Or some shifter muscle at your side. We birds of prey have our own set of skills and duties. I'd like to offer you my services, to make sure this goes down the way you want it to."

The Master seemed a little taken aback, but the fey knight was all smiles. Tony appeared to take his cue from Duncan and welcomed Joe's help.

It didn't take much longer before the Master vampire, fey knight, and owl shifter were on their way, no doubt heading to Tony's lair in the city. The Redstone brothers got to work while they waited for a ride, sorting through the rubble that was all that was left of the once-elegant wine bar.

"Melissa's going to have a cow when she sees this," Miranda said, looking at the devastation.

"Don't worry." Mag's arms came around her from behind, already making her feel better. "It just so happens I know a really good construction company that will work for cheap."

"Really?" Miranda turned in his arms, excited by the idea that his family would help hers. "I didn't think Redstone Construction took on such small jobs."

"You'd be surprised." Bob smiled as he intruded on their conversation. He walked past them holding a giant section of the broken bar over his head to put on the growing pile of debris in the center of the room.

"We do all kinds of construction from home remodels to office towers and everything in between," Mag replied, pulling her closer in his arms and smiling in a mischievous way. "Of course, usually, you have to know somebody to get on our short list. People have been known to wait a year or more for one of our specialty crews to become available."

"Oh…" Miranda understood his game. It felt good to be able to laugh with him now that the danger had passed. "I think I *do* know somebody who could help. Imagine that."

They didn't get to say anything more because Steve arrived, jingling keys in his hand. He crept carefully through what was left of the glass door and whistled.

"Damn," he commented. "You guys sure made a mess in here." Steve looked around, casting his gaze on each one of his brothers and Miranda. "Everybody all right?"

"We're good," Bob answered quickly. "But you missed all the action. You're not going to believe what happened here."

"Tell me on the way home. The outer door looks solid enough to secure the place for the night. We'll organize a crew to come back tomorrow and start cleaning this place up." He looked around, his gaze critical. "Or finish tearing it down," he added. "We might have to start from scratch here."

"Is Melissa okay?" Miranda moved toward Steve, Mag at her side.

"Safe and sound. Currently drinking hot toddies with Lindsey at Grif's place. She's handling herself well. Took Joe's shapeshifting fine, all things considered."

"I figured she'd seen that," Mag added. "And she saw a hell of a lot over at Raintree's, Miranda." The other men gathered by the door and started heading out to the big SUV Steve had brought with him, but Miranda and Mag stopped for a moment.

"What exactly happened there?" Miranda asked, her gaze worried.

"Nothing bad happened to Mel," Mag was quick to say. "She was tied up in one of the back rooms. They vamp with her was having dinner. A half-naked human chick from the club. Mel saw him bite her. And then I rushed in and knocked him out. The girl fled and I was able to free Melissa. We were on our way out when Raintree blocked our path."

"And Mag was a blur when he staked the bastard," Bob put in rather loudly from the doorway. "Come on, you two. You can talk on the way."

Mag laughed and Miranda went along with him as he led her out the door. Bob locked up, turning the bottom latch before closing the door. There was a better lock, but it needed a key and really, there was nothing worth stealing inside anymore. It would have to do until repairs could be made.

"You killed Raintree?" Miranda asked once they were in the dark embrace of the SUV's large cabin.

"Yep." Mag would not apologize for ending that low life bastard. He had deserved what he'd gotten. The minute he'd messed with Miranda's family, he was toast as far as Mag was concerned.

"You should have seen him, Miranda," Bob added, ever the loquacious brother. "He was so fast! I've never seen anyone move like that before. Raintree didn't know what hit him. It was merciful, in a way. One minute he was there, threatening all of us. The next, he was staked to a cinder block wall, no threat to anyone ever again."

"Forgive him," Mag sent his thoughts soundlessly to his mate. *"Bob can be a bit of a pain in the ass sometimes, but we love him anyway."*

Miranda sent amusement through their connection. *"It's okay. I'm just glad none of you were hurt. Have I thanked you for saving my grandniece yet?"* She moved closer to him on the bench seat they shared, snuggling into his arms.

"I think you just did. But if you want to do it some more, I'll be happy to entertain your thanks...the minute we're alone." He

squeezed her, the cat inside him reveling at the feel of his mate in his arms.

"Done," she quipped, reaching up to give him a peck on the cheek.

Steve drove them to Grif's house where Miranda was reunited with a slightly tipsy Melissa. They hugged and Mel cried a bit, but she soon recovered. Mag watched over the reunion with a patient gaze while he passed on the Master vampire's words of warning to Grif. He let his brothers fill Grif in on Duncan's appearance and how the battle in the bar had gone.

The men were gathered in the kitchen while the women had retreated to the living room. Mag kept watch from the hallway, adding his thoughts to his brothers' report when necessary, but otherwise keeping tabs on the ladies. His lady in particular.

He liked that. *His* lady.

"And you're my *guy."* Miranda's thought sounded in his mind.

Damn. He loved their ability to speak silently, but it still caught him off-guard.

"You'll get used to it in time," she offered.

"I guess so," he agreed. *"How's Mel taking all this?"*

"A lot better than I thought she would. She knows I'm a bloodletter and I'm about to tell her she's my niece. Wish me luck."

Mag watched as Miranda took a deep breath and forged on. The revelation went well, he could see, when Mel launched herself into Miranda's arms for a giant, teary hug. Smiles all around told him that things were going to be okay with Miranda's family.

In fact, things were looking up everywhere. No shifters had been harmed in the evening's action and a few very bad apples had been eliminated permanently from the bloodletters' ranks. All in all, a good outcome. Especially since the biggest threat to his mate had been forever neutralized. Cassie was gone, and with her, the vindictiveness that had made her target Miranda for so very long.

Miranda was finally free of the burden of how she'd been made immortal. Free of the specter that had haunted her path for so long. It was a new beginning for her—and for them as a couple.

They spent an hour or so at Grif's house before it came time to leave. They had to get home to their light-proofed house in the desert before the sun rose for Miranda's safety. Otherwise, he was certain the women would have talked for several more hours.

They left with promises to get together the next evening at the bar. Mag had talked with his brothers about getting a work crew out there early the next morning so the place was at least a little cleaned up before the women got there. Grif had agreed. His mate, Lindsey, had invited Melissa to stay with them so she could rest a bit before heading back into the city, and Mel had taken them up on the offer.

Everybody was safe, and when Mag pulled the borrowed car into his drive, he was glad to see the raptor on the roof who hooted the all clear. His house was secure. He was never more glad to lock the doors, arm the security system, and head for the bedroom with his mate.

They'd been through the wringer that night, but they stopped in the master bath for a quick shower before laying down. Mag pulled his sleepy vampiress into his arms, and they both fell asleep.

Mag woke only a few hours later. It was about noon. Miranda would sleep the rest of the day, but shifters didn't require much sleep. He went into his office and started making plans…and calls.

One of the guys who was cleaning up at the bar did some measuring, and Mag started laying out a drawing of the bar's dimensions. From there, he started creating a new design for the interior layout and sourcing different finish options. He'd leave the froufrou work up to the ladies in picking colors and linens and such, but he could show them options for different types of stone or millwork at least. It wasn't his usual kind of project, but he enjoyed the hours he spent on it, knowing it just might make his mate smile.

That night when Miranda woke, they made love, long and slow. He wanted to savor his time with his mate, and she seemed to feel the same. They rolled around on the big bed, first with him on top, then her, then back to him. The one constant was the fact that they were joined—body and soul. Their minds were linked and they could anticipate each other's desires and wishes.

It was a hell of a way to make love. And, Mag realized, he only had this with Miranda. He had only ever had this with Miranda. Without her, he would never have this again. It would be his honor and duty to keep her safe for the rest of their days.

"That goes both ways," she reminded him, picking up on his thoughts again as they came down from the highest peak yet.

"I love you, Miranda." He kissed her gently.

"And I love you, Magnus Redstone. My One."

EPILOGUE

Miranda handed over her notes to the Alpha sometime later. She hadn't forgotten her promise to do so in all the tumult, but it had taken her some time to organize her thoughts into a format other people could understand. She'd taken pains to remember everything she could about her time as a captive of the mage. She'd written it all down and organized what she could of the things he'd said about the *Venifucus* and their plans.

Handing it over to Grif was a big step. She'd made copies, of course. She kept one for herself and gave the other to the Master. Duncan had asked for a copy as well, so she'd made another for the fey knight.

In fact, all three powerful men gathered in Grif's kitchen so she could go over her notes with them. She answered their questions as best she could, but a lot of what the mage had said still didn't make any sense to her. She left the meeting feeling glad that she'd been able to give them something. Maybe it wouldn't be useful after all, but at least she'd tried.

Mag took her home after the meeting and they made love, helping her erase the memories of the evil mage and her time in captivity.

The meeting of minds at Grif's house went on for a while

after Miranda and Mag left, though. All three men wore troubled gazes as they went over her notes.

"Miranda did a good job of organizing this," Tony offered at last, when he'd finished reading through it all for the third time.

"She did," Duncan agreed. "But that still doesn't make this information any easier to read. I fear it indicates the worst is yet to come."

"Yeah." Grif sat back in his chair and stretched, rubbing his eyes. "That's what I get from it too. Not good news at all."

"We'll have to redouble our efforts," Duncan said finally, his voice grim. "We'll have to be ready when the shit hits the fan."

Grif almost laughed at the ancient fey warrior using modern slang. It sounded funny coming out of his mouth when most of the time, the guy sounded like a living antique. But this was no laughing matter. The *Venifucus* were on the move, and it could be a big problem for every living being in the mortal realm. Grif's duty was clear.

"We'll prepare, but we should talk to the Lords. They've been gathering intel on the *Venifucus* for a lot longer than we have here in Las Vegas. They've got a farther reach even than Redstone Construction. If I'm going to put my resources at their disposal, I think I'm going to have to send someone up there to be our on-the-spot liaison."

And he had just the brother in mind...

# # #

191

ABOUT THE AUTHOR

Bianca D'Arc has run a laboratory, climbed the corporate ladder in the shark-infested streets of lower Manhattan, studied and taught martial arts, and earned the right to put a whole bunch of letters after her name, but she's always enjoyed writing more than any of her other pursuits. She grew up and still lives on Long Island, where she keeps busy with an extensive garden, several aquariums full of very demanding fish, and writing her favorite genres of paranormal, fantasy and sci-fi romance.

Bianca loves to hear from readers and can be reached through Twitter (@BiancaDArc), Facebook (BiancaDArcAuthor) or through the various links on her website.

WELCOME TO THE D'ARC SIDE…
WWW.BIANCADARC.COM

OTHER BOOKS BY BIANCA D'ARC

Now Available

Brotherhood of Blood
One & Only
Rare Vintage
Phantom Desires
Sweeter Than Wine
Forever Valentine
Wolf Hills
Wolf Quest

Tales of the Were
Lords of the Were
Inferno

Tales of the Were – The Others
Rocky
Slade

*Tales of the Were – Redstone
Clan*
Grif
Red
Magnus

Guardians of the Dark
Half Past Dead
Once Bitten, Twice Dead
A Darker Shade of Dead
The Beast Within
Dead Alert

Gifts of the Ancients
Warrior's Heart

String of Fate: Cat's Cradle

Dragon Knights
Maiden Flight
The Dragon Healer
Border Lair
Master at Arms
The Ice Dragon
Prince of Spies
Wings of Change
FireDrake
Dragon Storm
Keeper of the Flame

Resonance Mates
Hara's Legacy
Davin's Quest
Jaci's Experiment
Grady's Awakening

Jit'Suku Chronicles
Arcana: King of Swords
Arcana: King of Cups
Arcana: King of Clubs
End of the Line
Sons of Amber: Ezekiel
Sons of Amber: Michael

StarLords: Hidden Talent

Print Anthologies
Ladies of the Lair
I Dream of Dragons Vol. 1
Brotherhood of Blood
Caught by Cupid

OTHER BOOKS BY BIANCA D'ARC

(continued)

Coming Soon

Resonance Mates
Harry's Sacrifice
eBook Release: March 11, 2014
Print Release: March 2015

String of Fate #2
King's Throne
April 2014

Tales of the Were - Redstone Clan #4
Bobcat
Spring 2014

Jit'Suku Chronicles ~ Arcana #4
King of Stars
Summer 2014

Tales of the Were - Redstone Clan #5
Matt
Summer 2014

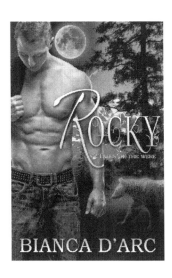

TALES OF THE WERE – THE OTHERS
ROCKY
BY BIANCA D'ARC

On the run from her husband's killers, there is only one man who can help her now… her Rock.

Maggie is on the run from those who killed her husband nine months ago. She knows the only one who can help her is Rocco, a grizzly shifter she knew in her youth. She arrives on his doorstep in labor with twins. Magical, shapeshifting, bear cub twins destined to lead the next generation of werecreatures in North America.

Rocky is devastated by the news of his Clan brother's death, but he cannot deny the attraction that has never waned for the small human woman who stole his heart a long time ago. Rocky absented himself from her life when she chose to marry his childhood friend, but the years haven't changed the way he feels for her.

And now there are two young lives to protect. Rocky will do everything in his power to end the threat to the small family and claim them for himself. He knows he is the perfect Alpha to teach the cubs as they grow into their power… if their mother will let him love her as he has always longed to do.

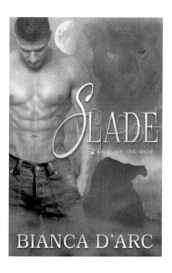

TALES OF THE WERE – THE OTHERS
SLADE
BY BIANCA D'ARC

The fate of all shifters rests on his broad shoulders, but all he can think of is her.

Slade is a warrior and spy sent to Nevada to track a brutal murderer before the existence of all shifters is revealed to a world not ready to know.

Kate is a priestess serving the large community of shifters that have gathered around the Redstone cougars. When their matriarch is murdered and the scene polluted by dark magics, she knows she must help the enigmatic man sent to track the killer.

Together, Slade and Kate find not one but two evil mages that they alone can neutralize. Slade finds it hard to keep his hands off his sexy new partner, the cougars are out for blood, and the killers have an even more sinister plan in mind.

Can Kate somehow keep her hands to herself when the most attractive man she's ever met makes her want to throw caution to the wind? And can Slade do his job and save the situation when he's finally found a woman who can make him purr?

TALES OF THE WERE – REDSTONE CLAN
GRIF
BY BIANCA D'ARC

Griffon Redstone is the eldest of five brothers and the leader of one of the most influential shifter Clans in North America. He seeks solace in the mountains, away from the horrific events of the past months, for both himself and his young sister. The deaths of their older sister and mother have hit them both very hard.

Lindsey Tate is human, but very aware of the werewolf Pack that lives near her grandfather's old cabin. She's come to right a wrong her grandfather committed against the Pack and salvage what's left of her family's honor—if the wolves will let her. Mostly, they seem intent on running her out of town on a rail.

But the golden haired stranger, Grif, comes to her rescue more than once. He stands up for her against the wolf Pack and then helps her fix the old generator at the cabin. When she performs a ceremony she expects will end in her death, the shifter deity has other ideas. Thrown together by fate, neither of them can deny their deep attraction, but will an old enemy tear them apart?

Warning: Frisky cats get up to all sorts of naughtiness, including a frenzy-induced multi-partner situation that might be a little intense for some readers.

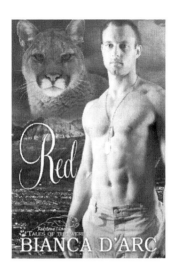

TALES OF THE WERE – REDSTONE CLAN
RED
BY BIANCA D'ARC

A water nymph and a werecougar meet in a bar fight… No joke.

Steve Redstone agrees to keep an eye on his friend's little sister while she's partying in Las Vegas. He's happy to do the favor for an old Army buddy. What he doesn't expect is the wild woman who heats his blood and attracts too much attention from Others in the area.

Steve ends up defending her honor, breaking his cover and seducing the woman all within hours of meeting her, but he's helpless to resist her. She is his mate and that startling fact is going to open up a whole can of worms with her, her brother and the rest of the Redstone Clan.

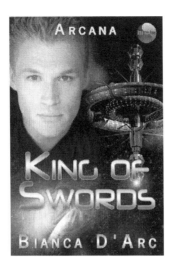

KING OF SWORDS
BY BIANCA D'ARC
Arcana, Book 1

David is a newly retired special ops soldier, looking to find his way in an unfamiliar civilian world. His first step is to visit an old friend, the owner of a bar called *The Rabbit Hole* on a distant space station. While there, he meets an intriguing woman who holds the keys to his future.

Adele has a special ability, handed down through her family. Adele can sometimes see the future. She doesn't know exactly why she's been drawn to the space station where her aunt deals cards in a bar that caters to station workers and ex-military. She only knows that she needs to be there. When she meets David, sparks of desire fly between them and she begins to suspect that he is part of the reason she traveled halfway across the galaxy.

Pirates gas the inhabitants of the station while Adele and David are safe inside a transport tube and it's up to them to repel the invaders. Passion flares while they wait for the right moment to overcome the alien threat and retake the station. But what good can one retired soldier and a civilian do against a ship full of alien pirates?

31240013R00116

Made in the USA
Lexington, KY
05 April 2014